SHADOW WALKER

THE BEGINNING
CORD OF THREE STRANDS

Marion David Russell

Situations come along life's path when we need a little help from family and friends. People need to know that they have the ability and resources to meet every challenge that life brings and that they do not need to face these challenges alone.

SHADOW WALKER

Marion David Russell

Book previously
published by Tate Publishing, LLC
Cover and interior design by "Dexter Wolfe"
Illustrations by "Barbara 'Joanna Rue' Russell (author's granddaughter)"

Published in the United States of America

ISBN: 9798738905667

INTRODUCTION

Shadow Walker is based on a dream about my grandchildren on an adventure.

What if . . .
The unseen could be seen?

By faith he left Egypt, not fearing the wrath of the king; for he persevered, as though seeing Him who is unseen.
Hebrews 11:27

One who dwells in the shelter of the Most High
Will lodge in the shadow of the Almighty.
Psalms 91:1

Two are better than one because they have a good return for their labor; for if either of them falls, the one will lift up his companion. But woe to the one who falls when there is not another to lift him up! Furthermore, if two lie down together they keep warm, but how can one be warm *alone*? And if one can overpower him who is alone, two can resist him. A cord of three *strands* is not quickly torn apart.
Ecclesiastes 4:9-12

FORWARD

I was, and still am, a silly little girl. I have always had a vivid imagination. Luckily, God blessed me with parents who let me explore that imagination, and sisters who would tag along for the adventure. My adventures frequented the areas of princess and magical lands, often fueled by Disney stories. I remember creating Goldadot with my sisters: a magical land that you could only get to by crossing through the middle of the mirror tree in our backyard. Looking back, the mirror tree wasn't all that magical. It was simply two redbud trees that had intertwined themselves to shape what appeared to be a standing mirror, which became more predominant as they grew. However, despite how un-magical the trees were, my sisters and I would cross over into that land and be heroines. The three of us girls ruled Goldadot. And, with our many rules, I'm positive it was impossible to stay out of trouble in Goldadot. We even catalogued the daily tasks in a notebook given to us by my great grandmother. We could fine people, or send them to the dungeon. We had servants, and people to cater to our every need. We were astonishing. And I was important. I think that's what all people long for: to be something above the mundane, to forget momentarily that they are only human, and, when possible, live beyond those repetitive daily tasks.

Unfortunately, we tend to forget that being human is extraordinary. To be human is to be created in the image of God. Even the angels can't claim that. God looks upon us with love and longs for us to have a relation-ship with him. He provides us with purpose. He gives us the strength to be more than we can imagine. *Shadow Walker* shows us exactly that. We get to be exceptional right where we are. As God's creation and desire, we are extraordinary.

Shadow Walker reminds me of the times that my sisters and I pretended in the backyard. It reminds me of the times in my life when I've used my imagination to temporarily escape from the world. But it also shows me that I don't have to escape to be spectacular. It is within all Christians to be exactly what God created us to be, right where we are. "For God did not give us a spirit of timidity, but of power, of love and self-discipline" (2 Timothy 1:7). What we desire we already have. It just takes some time living and walking in his shadow to come to realize that fact.

—*Brittany Suzanne Werner*

PROLOGUE

CHAPTER 1

A full moon hung low over the lake where Tommy and his grandfather had fished that day. Silhouettes of trees reaching upward sliced moonbeams into long strips of light that gently vanished into the night air. A host of night creatures sang praises to the Creator of evening and morning, as Tommy and his

1

grandfather sat watching and listening to a masterpiece in the making.

"Well, son, it's bedtime." The old gentleman leaned forward and with a low moan rose to his feet. An aged black and white border collie raised his head to see what the elderly man was doing.

"Aw, Grandpa, I'm not even sleepy yet."

"You never are the first night you're here." Grandpa smiled and put his ruddy hand on the young man's shoulder. The old dog watched their every move. "Come on, Butch." Slowly, and with great effort, the gray-faced dog got to his feet and lumbered toward the door. "Ol' Butch is getting slower than I am, Tommy." They both smiled as they waited for Butch to make his way from the other end of the porch. Tommy patted the dog's head, and the three walked inside.

Tommy made his way toward the fireplace where reddened embers glowed beneath a popping log. In moments, the flames lapping around the wood mesmerized him. The dying log's warmth added to the hypnotic effect.

"Bedtime, son." A low somber voice broke the young man's trance.

"But it's early yet, and I'm not sleepy," he said as the warmth of the fire brought a yawn with Tommy's protest.

"We have an early rise, a full day of fishing, and chores around the cabin. We both need our rest."

After making several circles on his rug, and with a similar low grown like Grandpa made at the swing, Butch found just the right spot, plopped down, and settled in for the evening. Tommy chuckled at the dog and made his way across the cabin to an aged green army cot and sleeping bag.

The evening was young, and the elderly man knew what was coming next.

"Grandpa, will you tell me a story?"

The old man looked at the clock, smiled broadly, and pulled his lumpy, stuffed chair closer to the cot. The noise from the chair's legs scraping on the floor startled the dog. Tommy rolled out his sleeping bag on the cot and began changing into his nightclothes.

"Hmmm…then you will go to bed?"

"I promise."

Tommy crawled into his sleeping bag and propped himself up on one elbow, chin in hand. He focused on the kind, wrinkled face whose broad nose supported narrow reading glasses. The wire rims twinkled in the moving firelight.

Grandpa sat down and leaned back in the chair, thought for a moment, then said, "I don't think I have ever told you the story about Noble. He was a young man, about your age, and was like most young men that you would know. You would not especially notice him in a crowd or name him as one who would most likely be president some day. He grew up in a rural area not far from a big city. Born to young parents just starting out, he would be considered poor by some standards. He liked to do most things that young men do, but most of all he liked to dream. Having a healthy imagination when you don't have a lot of things can be very entertaining."

"Did he have video games?"

"No," smiled Grandpa, "He didn't have video games." Grandpa knew that Tommy was jesting with that question. He gave the boy a look, cleared his throat, and continued.

"In his favorite dreams, he would be someone unique. He would not necessarily be a superhero with great powers, just someone unusual. These dreams could be daydreams or at nighttime, but he always remembered the dreams. They did not make Noble act weird, but he did believe that he was someone exceptional. Tommy, is it weird to believe that you're different from your friends?"

Grandpa leaned forward and in a softer tone asked, "What would it be like if all your friends were just like you? Is it your unusual friends that make life interesting? It's our differences that make us interesting to one another, isn't it?" Grandpa leaned back in his chair and paused for a moment. He could tell Tommy was thinking about what he had just said.

"You know, I think you're right, Grandpa. Josh Winkler is really different from all my other friends, but I think I like him the best."

"Josh Winkler, huh? What's so different about Josh?"

"He tells neat stories. Some of the kids tease him about his stories and call him names, like space alien or freak. But I like his stories and I like Josh."

Grandpa continued. "Now, Tommy, I don't want to paint a rosy picture or lead you to believe that Noble had a fairytale life. As I mentioned before, his parents married very young. Son, life can be very cruel at times, especially to the very young and to the old. He experienced divorce, as many do, even before he could understand what it was. Again, Grandpa paused, and then asked Tommy, "Do you understand divorce?"

"Not really. I hear some of the older kids at school talk about it."

Grandpa thought for a moment, and then came up with a good way to help Tommy identify with Noble and divorce.

"I know that you remember how much time you spent with me and your Grandmother while your parents were finishing their college degrees. What if they never came to take you home? What if they just left you with us and never came to see you? That's what it was like for Noble and his father. Does this help?"

"Oh. Okay. Some of my friends talk about their dad or mom that they never see. I remember missing dad and mom sometimes when staying with you."

"Imagine how Noble felt. His father now lived far away and he hardly ever saw him. Noble felt alone and scared. He missed his father. The main thing that helped Noble fill the absence of his dad was learning that he had a heavenly father who would always be with him. Finding faith in that heavenly father helped him overcome most of the fear, but there's a place in a young man's heart that only 'dad' can fill. But, his mother met a man who became like a father to Noble. Do your friends ever talk about step dads or step mothers?"

"Sometimes I hear other kids call their dads by first name. Is that because he's not their real dad?"

"Most of the time, but not always, a child can have a close relationship with a real parent or a stepparent. Both Noble and his step dad chose to be close. It also helps if you like some of the same things. Noble and his step dad both like the outdoors, especially fishing, like you and I do, Tommy. A fishing trip's where Noble's adventure begins."

5

Tommy's interest perked when his Grandpa mentioned a fishing trip. He was now sitting on the cot with his arms and legs crossed as his Grandpa continued.

FISHING TRIP

CHAPTER 2

Noble had reached his teenage years before his parents could afford what we'll call a real vacation. A two-week fishing trip to places they had planned to see for years began one summer on a Saturday morning. Because they were in no real hurry, and after driving for a while, they stopped at a roadside rest that overlooked a beautiful valley. Picnic tables under a wooden shelter provided a perfect spot to enjoy a sparrow hawk circling high above grassy fields, bordered by tree-fenced lines. In the distance, two large barns sat to the right of a picturesque farmhouse poised on a gently sloping knoll. A narrow stream sliced through the fields and wound its way into a heavily wooded area that lay toward the right of their view. Noble and his parents enjoyed the scenery while eating lunch.

Noble's father headed for the vending area that was past the visitors building and restrooms on the far end of the roadside rest toward the wooded area. Because his father was gone for a very long time, Noble and his mother went to look for him. Checking the vending area and the restroom, they began calling to him. Noble's mother knew that her husband was a practical joker. They both expected him to jump out and scare them at any time.

"Dad does that to mom," Tommy chuckled, "and it's so funny when she jumps."

Grandpa smiled, visualizing his startled daughter. "I'm sure that she enjoys that. And Noble's mother would have enjoyed the practical joke, too. But it didn't happen."

"John Robert!" she called

Noble laughed. That's what she called her husband when she was upset with him. *He's in big trouble now.*

"Dad! Come on. Let's go fishing!" Noble yelled.

"John Robert! This isn't funny anymore. Get out here!"

The more they called and the longer they searched, Noble could tell in his mother's voice that she was beyond mad. Her voice quivered when she yelled. They continued to search, but it seemed that he had vanished without a trace.

"I'm scared," she said finally, near tears.

His father was not at the vending area or anywhere to be found. While Noble expanded his search of the area, his mother hurried to the visitor's building to call for help.

Past the vending area towards the woods, he noticed a footpath that headed down into the valley toward the stream and turned into the woods.

"Maybe Dad went to look for a fishing hole," Noble yelled back at his mother, but she had disappeared into the building.

Following the path for what seemed to be a long time, he noticed a tall stone wall through the trees on his right. *Visiting an old fort on this trip would be a real bonus*, he thought. As the path began to turn away from the stream and toward the wall, a large wooden door came into sight. Something lay on the ground in front of the door. As he hurried closer, he could see that it was his father's fishing hat.

"Why would he go in there?" he muttered, as if asking the hat when he picked it up. The door was not completely shut. Leaning on it with all his weight, the door opened enough for him to look in. He called for his father, but not too loudly.

"Dad!" he called a second time, moving his head closer to the opening, but again no answer. Applying his weight to the door again, it began to slowly swing open by itself. When the door came to a stop, he called again. No answer, no echo, nothing, as if the huge door absorbed his voice.

Noble began to talk to himself. "Why would anyone want to go in this place alone? If the door would happen to close, I don't think I could pull it open. But Dad may be hurt. I need to go see."

Before entering the door, Noble checked the path he came down to see if help was coming. He found a large stone that he wedged in front of the door to keep it open. Checking the path again, Noble turned toward the door and entered. The inside of the walled area did not look much different than the outside. *Maybe a little darker*, he thought. Noble felt strange, but his concern was for his father. "I'm going to see someone very soon. Right, dad?" Noble said aloud, anticipating his father's sudden appearance from behind a tree or bush. However, the farther he walked, the more he wondered why his father would go so far without telling them where he was going. *Very strange*, thought Noble.

Speaking of strange, he noticed that the odd feeling was a little stronger. It was kind of a good feeling, like telling the truth when you know that you're in trouble.

Tommy smiled and nodded in agreement. "You mean like when I broke Mom's vase and could have blamed it on the cat but didn't?"

Grandpa smiled and winked at Tommy. "Exactly," he continued.

At first, Noble walked slowly and as quietly as possible down the winding path lined with shrubs, bushes, and trees. With plenty of places to hide, he expected at any moment to hear, "Got ya!" and his father's laughter. Eyes darting from side to side, watching for any movement, as well as listening for the snap of a twig or the rustle of leaves, he continued to explore the path. But the further away from the door, the more he identified with his mother's fear.

This isn't right. Dad's a joker, but he isn't mean. He wouldn't scare us like this. Something's wrong.

Noble quickened his pace. Thoughts of his father being injured by an animal or beaten and robbed raced through his mind. He began to jog and shout for his father.

"Dad! Come out, please. Mom's scared and calling the police!"

Stopping only briefly to catch his breath, he would turn and look behind for any sign of his injured father. Becoming more convinced that something was wrong, he hoped that his father could jump out from a hiding place and scare him. At least then he would be okay and they could get out of this place and continue their vacation.

Fear and tension mounted, as he pressed onward.

"Come on, Dad! Please," Noble shouted, voice cracking with emotion and shortness of breath.

He had to stop again. His heart was pounding. He was gasping for breath and near tears. *Where is he? Did I miss him while running down the path? Should I go back and check?*

Turning around and looking behind, the scene looked much the same as it had since he entered. Trees and shrubs, a variety of greenery, and an empty path: nothing out of place or unusual for a wooded area.

Just a little further, and then I'm going back for help.

Noble turned and continued his search, running as far as he could and calling to his father as before. Just as he was about to return for help, something inside urged him forward. Pushing himself until he thought his chest would burst; he stopped and rested himself against a tree close to the path. Emotion finally ruled. Tears flowed as he questioned, *why's this happening? Where's Dad?*

He sat down to rest before heading back. As he sat with his head resting on his arms supported by his knees, visions of police and bloodhounds searching the woods for a body crushed his pounding heart. *He can't be gone. This has already happened once!*

When he stood up to go back the way he came, he caught a glimpse of something out of place through the trees. Moving further down the path, the 'something' came into view. He stopped and gazed in amazement. What he saw through the trees was the wall of a huge building. That was not all that seemed out of place.

As he moved closer, more buildings came into view. Once he cleared the trees, the path ended, and a city began.

Noble stopped at the end of the path. This was nothing like he had ever seen before. Towering brick buildings had been constructed right up against the forest. *Where am I?*

Stepping from a dirt path over a concrete curb, Noble stood in an empty street, trying to make sense of this place. Some of the larger buildings had beautiful architecture. Combinations of brick and stone outlined the corners as well as the windows and doorways. Some of the more decorative buildings had domed roofs. But most of the buildings were two or three story and rather plain.

Where are the people? Where are the cars and shoppers? A city in the middle of nowhere, and no people?

As he stood in the empty street, he observed street signs, light posts, business advertisement; most of the things you would expect to see in any city, except for people.

He began to walk slowly forward down a wide, broken pavement that separated the cracked sidewalks. Dark, almost black windows offered no reflections from the glass, like the light was absorbed. Some of the smaller buildings had bars on the doors and windows. You would expect to see trash in the streets and graffiti on the buildings if the city was abandoned, but there was none. Noble's concern for his father deepened as the massive city seemed to consume him. *How will I ever find my dad in this place, if he's here?* However, the concern for his father kept him going.

With no clue where to begin, Noble tried the door on the first building on his right. The door was locked. Knocking repeatedly without a response, he tried cupping his hands to the glass and his forehead and looking inside. The darkened glass prevented him from seeing inside the building.

"Hey! Is anyone in there! I'm looking for my dad! Can you help me?"

Noble tried the next building on the block without success. Crossing the street, he tried the first building to the left of the path. Knocking on the door and yelling for help ended as before: no response. Moving to building number four, he pulled the handle and the door moved, but only far enough for Noble to see that the door was chained from the inside. Looking in, the room was practically empty. He could see a bar and some tables and chairs. *This must have been some sort of place to eat.*

Walking up the sidewalk to the next building, he crossed an alley. Glancing down the alley, he thought he saw something move between the buildings. Standing in the alley for a minute or so, hoping that someone would emerge, he finally moved to the door of the next building.

Knocking and calling as before, and with the same results, he moved toward the next doorway. The building sat on the corner of the first intersection. From his viewpoint, it appeared that the entrance was located at the corner, on an angle. Becoming more anxious with every locked door and the seemingly insurmountable odds of finding his father anytime soon, a glimmer of hope poked its head around the corner and then quickly disappeared.

"Hey! Wait!" Noble ran, turned the corner, and stopped. A small group of people not much taller than him hurried down the street. "Hey! I'm looking for my dad! Can you help me, please?" Calling to them again, they didn't stop or look back. He ran after them and continued calling out for them to stop.

At the next intersection, some of the group turned left, some crossed the street straight ahead, and some crossed diagonally. *Great. Which group do I follow?* Noble chose to follow the group that crossed diagonally. Already exhausted from the path, he finally had to break off the pursuit. He walked to the corner where the group he was following had made a left turn. Turning the corner, the area ahead to the right looked more residential. A few two story framed houses were mixed in with the brick buildings. *This looks promising. I'll try some of the houses.*

Crossing the street and coming to the first framed house, he noticed bars on the doors and windows, like those he saw on some of the brick buildings. Knocking on the door and calling for help ended as before. Trying the next residence ended the same. A mixture of frustration, anger, and fear for his father's safety was bringing Noble to his wits end. *I have to stay calm and keep looking. And remember my way out.*

Moving further into what looked more like a residential part of the city, he could see people moving about but never getting close enough to speak. When Noble approached the people, they would hurry away. He would call to them, but they would not answer. He tried stepping in front of them to see if they would stop. But they turned around, changed direction, and never broke stride, mumbling to themselves.

"Must hide, stranger in town," he heard one of them say.

"Doomed! Doomed, I tell you!" said another. Noble thought that they must have seen his father, but why were they so afraid?

As he continued stepping in front of them, trying to get one of them to stop and talk, he got a good look at some of their faces. They appeared old but young at the same time. He did not see wrinkles of age on their faces, but age in their expression, like they had been in fear or dread for a long time. All the people that Noble encountered were dressed in robes that tied at the waist: gray, dreary-looking robes that blended in with the color of the buildings.

What a strange bunch. As he searched on into the city, he continued in vain to question the strange little people about his father.

THE CITY

CHAPTER 3

"Now, son," Grandpa continued, "please don't be misled about this feeling Noble encountered when he walked through the door in the wall and began his search for his father. This feeling was not magic or anything of the sort. When he entered through the door, he took no thought for himself; that is, he considered someone else more important than himself. He stepped out of his comfort zone, out of his own little world to help someone else. Tommy, do you think we could call this a step of faith?"

Tommy thought for a moment. "Is this like helping your sister clean her room when you really don't want to and knowing that she won't help you clean yours?"

Grandpa leaned back in his chair and laughed out loud.

Butch woke up and looked at the two, maybe somewhat annoyed.

"Something like that. Noble acted upon the principle in Scripture that teaches us to consider others more important than self. In doing so, a power other than his own came to oversee his adventure.

Moving deeper into the city, Noble noticed a building that was different from the others. It was bright looking, clean, and had no bars on the doors or windows. Light glowed from within.

"Maybe these people can tell me what's going on, if they will talk to me," Noble said, now talking to himself aloud and becoming more frustrated with the lack of cooperation.

"Tommy, do you remember the problems you had when you changed schools last year?"

Tommy nodded. "Some of the kids didn't treat me very nice."

"No, they didn't. Change can be hard. Noble learned just like you did that with any change in life a struggle can be expected." Butch headed for the door. Tommy hopped off the cot to let him out.

"Keep going, Grandpa, I'm listening," Tommy hurriedly jumped back onto the cot.

Noble headed for what looked like a very large, two-story house. The people he saw around the building seemed calmer than those he first encountered. They dressed in a variety of clothing, and the expressions on their faces were more relaxed. When he approached, they turned to greet him and welcomed him in for a rest and some refreshment.

What a difference, Noble thought to himself. The people smiled and continued greeting their guest.

The beautiful carved double doors at the side of the building opened. Light from within beckoned Noble to enter. Noble gladly accepted their hospitality. A tall, slim man dressed in a white hooded robe, tied at the waist with a golden sash greeted him at the door and escorted Noble down a wide hallway. On the left side of the hallway were dormitory-like rooms filled with cheerful people making beds and folding clothes. On the right side was a large kitchen area where some great smelling food was being prepared. Singing could be heard with every step he took. The hallway opened into a room full of tables and chairs.

Once Noble was seated, the tall, slim man said, "You may stay as long as it takes to find the answers you seek." He then disappeared back down the hallway.

Noble was then served some of that great smelling food. A young couple sat a bowl of stew and fresh baked bread in front of him. A tray with some dark colored preserves, silverware, and napkins sat in the center of the table. As he began to eat, several of the younger residents joined him. He introduced himself and began asking questions.

"My name's Noble. I'm here looking for my dad. Have any of you seen a stranger come in here?"

"Nice to meet you, Noble," said the young man across the table. "I haven't seen anyone new but you. Sorry. I'm Eli. This is Kim," turning to the young woman setting next to him, "and that's Joanna Rue that just sat down next to you."

"Rue will be fine, Eli, thank you," she said pertly.

Noble turned to see an attractive young woman smiling at him. Leaning forward with her arms crossed and elbows resting on the table, the tilt of her head caused her shoulder length dark hair to curl under her chin. Her light olive complexion and deep brown eyes grabbed his attention. He didn't know how long he sat staring, but when she spoke, there was a hint of laughter in her greeting.

"Hi, Noble." She turned slightly toward him, unfolded her arms, and with elbows still on the table, rested her chin in her left hand and continued to smile.

Noble heard Eli and Kim chuckling. He realized what was happening and felt the heat in his face. He quickly turned toward the couple across the table.

"Nice to meet you, Eli and Kim. And thank you for making me feel welcome." He sat quietly for a moment before he spoke to Rue.

"It's nice to meet you too, Rue," he said finally, but with head down. "And I apologize for staring." He felt the heat return to his face.

"It's okay. Apology accepted. How can we help you? You mentioned as I was sitting down that you were looking for your dad."

"Yes. Dad, mom, and I were on vacation. We stopped at a roadside rest area. Dad went to the vending area and that's the last time mom and I saw him." Noble's emotion began to show as he thought about all that has happened. "I followed a path into the woods, thinking that he might be looking for a place to fish. I found his fishing hat lying in front of an open door in this huge wall. I followed the path looking for my dad and came to this city. I saw people who wouldn't help me …" his voice trailed off as his emotion welled. Noble fought to maintain his composure, but tears were flowing. He felt a hand on his shoulder.

"We'll help you find your dad," Rue assured him. "Come with me. Let's find a more private place to talk. Please excuse us Eli and Kim."

Noble followed Rue out of the large room, down a hallway that connected to stairs leading up to the second floor. They entered a room with a large, rectangular table lined with soft backed armless chairs.

"Have a seat," Rue directed as she closed the door.

Noble pulled a chair from the table and sat. Rue remained standing. She began to pace and had a thoughtful expression. Noble sat quietly, waiting and watching. He guessed that she was about his age, somewhere in her teens. She was about his height with a thin build. She wore tennis shoes, blue jeans, and a baggy gray sweatshirt.

"Okay." Rue slowly walked to the table and sat across from Noble. "You said that the door was open when you found your dad's hat. Correct?"

"Yes."

"And none of the people you saw would help you."

"No. They wouldn't even talk to me."

Rue sat quietly for a few moments. Her expression changed from puzzled to concern. "There's no good way to say this, so I'm just going to say it. Apparently your dad has been captured and brought into the city by force. The people you saw that wouldn't help you are called tormentors. They can't be trusted.

"No matter what you want from them, you won't get it, or they will do just the opposite of what you need," Rue explained.

Hearing the possibility that his father had been captured, Noble's emotions began to surface again. He sat with his eyes closed and took several deep breaths before regaining control. Opening his eyes, the expression on Rue's face looked as though she was about to join him with tears. They both sat quietly before continuing their conversation.

"How did these tormentors force my dad to come in here? He's twice their size and could have easily overpowered two or three of them."

"They appear small and weak by themselves, but when they work together, they're very powerful," answered Rue.

"Where did these tormentors take my dad?"

"Hard to say," she replied with a thoughtful pause. "It depends on which ones got him."

"Can you help me find him?"

"It's no use. Once you're in here, you cannot get free. If you leave, they will find you and bring you back. You can never be free of the tormentors." She responded with a hopeless tone in her voice.

"If you cannot beat them, then why were they afraid of my dad? When I tried to talk to them, they said, 'Stranger in the city. Must hide. Doomed, doomed!'" he explained.

"They're not afraid of your dad. They have him. They're afraid of you. You came into the city by choice to help another. It's you they fear. Just look at you." Rue gestured toward him with her hand as she spoke.

Noble could hardly believe that these tormentors would be afraid of him. What did she mean by "look at you?" He had not noticed the change in his appearance, being so caught up in the search for his father. The dark windows on the buildings gave no reflection when he walked by. What Noble saw as he looked at himself for the first time since he entered the city was amazing.

His first reaction was to look down. His clothes were brighter, stronger, and more rugged-looking than when he entered the city. On his feet were boots made for climbing and rugged terrain. His pants were heavy cloth, almost steel-like to the touch. Around his waist was a wide belt that carried a small sword. Over his shoulder in a leather pouch was a small oval shield. His upper body and arms were covered with material similar to his pants with the exception of his chest and back. These areas were covered more densely and heavily protected. When he felt around the belt toward the back, he found a helmet made of leather and flexible metal that fit him perfectly.

Tommy interrupted. "He sounds like one of my video game characters!"

"There you go. Now you have a picture in your mind of what Noble might have looked like." Tommy's excitement and growing interest in the story fueled Grandpa's creative abilities.

Noble jumped up from his chair, knocking it over backwards. Spinning, twisting, looking behind and over his shoulder, and muttering in broken sentences, Rue jumped from her seat and grabbed Noble by the shoulders.

"What's the matter with you?" she asked sternly.

The wide-eyed shock on Noble's face would have been humorous, had the situation not been so serious.

"What...how?" was all Noble could say as he stared wide-eyed at Rue. She let go of him and stepped back.

"What do you mean, 'What...how?'?"

"My clothes?" Noble stood with his arms away from his sides, looking down. "These are not the clothes I had on this morning."

"Do you mean to tell me that you changed your clothes and forgot that you did?" Rue was starting to enjoy this.

"No. I didn't change my clothes. I don't know how my clothes got changed!" Noble's voice was rising and he was breathing rapidly.

"Calm down. Take slow deep breaths."

Noble closed his eyes and took several deep breaths. *What kind of craziness is this? What's happening to me?*

"Come over here and sit down. I'm going to get us something to drink. Just relax. I'll be right back."

Rue picked up the chair Noble had knocked over and guided him into the seat. When she left the room, he leaned back in the chair and scooted down to lay his head back. The shield caught the chair. He reached over his shoulder and loosed it from its latch.

As he examined it, he noticed that inside the shield was written:

> *With all prayer and petition, pray at all times in the Spirit, and with this in view, be on the alert with all perseverance and petition for all the saints, and pray on my behalf, that utterance may be given to me in the opening of my mouth, to make known with boldness the mystery of the gospel, for which I am an ambassador in chains; that in proclaiming it I may speak boldly, as I ought to speak.*

The quote moved Noble's memory back to church camp. This was part of a letter written by Paul to one of the churches. He could not remember which one at the time, but he remembered that what he had read had to do with the armor that Paul told them that they would need to "stand and resist in the evil day". All he could say was "Wow!" If only he could savor the moment. Rue returned with two cups of water. She sat one on the table in front of Noble. She spoke to him, but he did not respond.

"I'll go with you," Rue repeated.

"What?" he said, half-listening.

"I'll go with you and help you find your dad, I said for the third time," she chided, acting put out.

"Oh! Yes! Sorry, I was a little sidetracked." He continued examining his shield and the rest of his armor.

"Was?" replied Rue. She turned and walked out of the room, still acting wounded. Suddenly he noticed that she was gone.

THE TEST BEGINS

CHAPTER 4

Realizing that he was alone, Noble went looking for Rue. He apologized again for ignoring her and thanked her for offering to help him. She acted like she did not hear him. As he stammered and stuttered, looking for the right words to bail himself out of trouble, she turned and said with a smile, "Welcome back."

Grandpa and Tommy were so into the story that they hadn't noticed the scratching on the door. Butch was literally put out and let them know how put out he was with a loud bark, snapping them both back to reality with a jerk.

"Speaking of welcome back ..." Tommy bolted from the cot to the door. The dog headed straight to the same spot and, with a similar moan as before, fell into place. Tommy was back on the cot as quickly as he went to the door. The actions of the boy and the dog were humorously pleasing to the elderly man. He took this opportunity to stretch a little.

"I'm ready, Grandpa."

"Okay. Give me a minute." Grandpa twisted from side to side a few times, sat down, and continued.

Noble realized that Rue was teasing. They had a good laugh and then it was down to the business of their plan of attack. The first problem was where to look. There were so many locations where the tormentors could have taken Noble's father; she did not know where to start. If she knew who had him, it would narrow the search. Each part of the city had different tormentors in control.

"One thing's for sure, we need a map. And I think I know where to find one," Rue called while striding toward the next room. At one time, she remembered seeing a map showing the locations of houses like hers. They were called safe houses. No one could find that map, but the head of the safe house mentioned a large old building in the city that looked like a church. We would call it the city building. The safe houses would probably not be marked on the city maps, but a map of the city would certainly help their journey. So Rue made preparations to leave with Noble and pick up a map.

When she returned to the room, Noble sat leaning forward, staring at the floor. When she entered, he looked up and saw the overnight bag slung over her shoulder. He looked back down at the floor as she approached.

"Why are you doing this?" he asked. "When I asked you to help me, I didn't mean for you to leave your home or your friends."

"How do you want me to help you?" She dropped her bag on the floor and sat on the arm of the chair.

"I don't know. Everything has happened so fast. My dad's missing and I have no idea what mom's doing. I don't even know what I'm doing. My clothes have change mysteriously and now a total stranger's willing to leave her home and help me. Why? What is this place? I don't even know where I am?"

"So many questions."

"Here's another one: the man in the white robe; he seated me and said, 'You may stay as long as it takes to find the answers you seek.' What does that mean? Answers to what questions? I don't even know what the questions are!"

"Okay. Okay, one question at a time. The man in the white robe that seated you is Ruach. Let me find him. He can answer your questions better than I can. Sit tight."

In a few minutes, Rue returned with Ruach.

"Noble, this is Ruach. Ask him your questions."

"Hello, Noble. How can I help you?" Ruach carried folding chairs from his office for him and Rue. Placing them in a semi-circle, Ruach and Rue sat down facing Noble, who had not moved since Rue left him.

Noble looked up and said, "Sir, I don't even know where to start."

Ruach smiled. "I understand. This has become a complicated place, but it hasn't always been this way. So, let me start and see if what I say answers some of your questions."

Ruach stood and paced slowly as he talked. "The city was once called Asphaleia, a beautiful city filled with strong families and many children. And for many generations they enjoyed the freedom of worshiping the creator of all things called the Higher Powers. The Higher Powers, being one in thought, body and being, allowed worshipers some creative license in building alters and places of worship, giving those gifts, abilities, and instruction on ways to please him. But, worshipers compromised their freedom, misused their gifts and abilities, and ignored his instruction by crafting images after their own imaginations. Hand cut stones unacceptable to the creator replaced uncut natural alters. Crafted images, half human, half beast, lined temples and corrupted natural high places of worship. The living creator was replaced by lifeless created images, powerless to direct the feet of the worshipers upon the path of life. With the passing of each generation, the compromises of the fathers were passed on to their children. The city once known as Asphaleia, a place of safety and security, became Sphallō, a place to trip up, and is now known as Peiratopos, a place of testing."

"So, I have entered a place of testing that used to be a safe place. What does that have to do with my dad missing and these strange clothes?" Noble asked.

"The clothes you will find very useful on your journey to find your father. Why the tormentors captured your father is anybody's guess. There's no rhyme or reason to what the tormentors do."

"Who are the tormentors? Where did they come from?"

"The tormentors were once guardians of the city. They now belong to Kuriopolis, the lord of the city."

"The lord of the city?"

"Yes. Kuriopolis came making big promises and great boasts. Asphaleia became known as Sphallō when many of the citizens as well as some of the guardians and overseers of the safe houses chose him as lord of the city. Eventually, these citizens became his captors or slaves. The guardians and overseers who blasphemed the Higher Powers by choosing Kuriopolis to rule the city became tormentors, the evil lord's minions, who used their gifts and abilities to harass or trip up good citizens and visitors like yourself."

Noble sat processing all of this information. *The lord of the city, tormentors, tests, all in a place I have never heard of.* While he sat trying to put his thoughts together, Rue thanked Ruach for his help.

"I know you were busy, Ruach. I think I can answer the rest of his questions," Rue said.

Rue returned to the arm of the chair as Ruach folded the chairs he brought and left the room. "Did that help any?" she asked.

"Maybe. Let's see. I have entered a city to be tested, ran by an evil lord who owns tormentors, who captures people for no apparent reason. Yah, I think I got it. Oh, I almost forgot. You get a free change of clothes for coming. This is insane!" Noble yelled.

"Calm down," Rue laughed. "Actually, that's a pretty good summary. And there's one more thing you need to know about the city. And that's where you are right now. You're in a safe house."

"What's a safe house? Does that mean that every place other than here's unsafe?"

"No," Rue laughed again. "There are other places in the city like this one. And we're going to find them. The citizens who live in the safe houses are good people. They help each other and are willing to help strangers like you. At one time, most of the city was like one big safe house. But the city changed. Evil, greed, and selfishness have lured citizens to make bad choices. Most of the good people have left or moved to a safe house."

"What prevents evil from overtaking the safe houses?"

"The people in the safe houses choose good over evil, and a power stronger than evil protects the safe house."

"And that brings me back to my first question. Why would you leave this protection to help a total stranger?"

"That's one of the answers you're going to have to seek. I have my reasons. Maybe I'll tell you and maybe I won't. Now, can we go get a map? Or, do you want to stay here where it's safe?" Rue picked up her bag and headed for the door. He was still sitting in the chair when she turned and said, "Well? Am I going alone?"

The city building was not far from their present location. It was an aged stone building with beautiful architecture. The building could be entered on any side by long stone stairways, leading visitors to groups of double doors with large stone columns on each side. Once through the doors, polished marble floors reflected a tall, arched ceiling covered with paintings of winged beasts. Consulting a directory on a wall, the two headed for the second floor. They were then directed to the city planner's office and were seated in front of the right person. When asked why they wanted maps of the city, Noble probably said too much.

"The Missing Persons Department is in a different building, and such matters should be handled by the police," said the person behind the desk.

They finally got their maps, but not before one of the officials on the top floor questioned them. Again, Noble explained his adventure, beginning at the rest stop. When he mentioned the safe house, the official turned his attention to Rue.

"Do you make it a habit to take up with strangers?"

"No," she answered in a tone that expressed some concern with the question.

"Why this one? Is it because he impressed you with his magic and his clothes? Or did he promise you power if—" asked the official, slightly raising his voice. Rue cut him off in a stronger voice, moving to the edge of her chair.

"He needed help! Is it now a crime to help someone?" Rue said.

"Don't get smart with me, young lady. Do you know who I am? I could have you both arrested!" the official replied.

"Arrest us? What? For looking for my dad?" Noble asked.

"Do you think that you're the first to come through here dressed the way you are? Your kind always causes trouble. You will turn this city upside down on your little mission," the official said, turning to Noble. Noble sat calmly while Rue became more irritated with the official. Noble noticed that her hand was white from gripping the arm of the chair.

She was about to speak, intending to direct the official's attention away from Noble and his armor, when Noble put his hand on her hand that was turning white from gripping the arm of the chair, as if to hold her back. He said calmly, "Sir, I will gladly wait here if you could find my dad and bring him to me so we could leave this city and continue our fishing trip."

"You would, would you? Well, that could be arranged. What's it worth to you? Would you donate your fancy clothes to the museum for the good of the whole city? Or maybe you could give them to me and I could donate them myself after I show them in my private collection for a while," said the official with a haughty smile and easing back in his chair.

Rue squirmed in her chair, glanced at Noble, and then looked intently at the official, thinking, *Is he for real? What's this meeting really about?* At the same time, Noble's suspicion was aroused, and he shifted forward in his chair. As he did, the sword caught the arm of the chair. He freed the sword with his hand while his mind was processing the official's proposition. When he grasped the sword, the thought came to him and he heard himself say, "The clothes are a gift and not a bargaining chip."

The official's expression changed from a smug grin to anger. "Why should a young punk like you have such a gift? You don't even know what to do with it. If I had it, I'd know what to do with it. Besides, you will never find your father unless you cooperate."

Rue was now on her feet, leaning across the desk, with her finger in the officials' face. "I don't care who you are. Noble's a guest in this city and you're an elected official.

You're a public servant and if you know anything about his father, it's your duty to tell him," she said emphatically.

The official jumped to his feet and slammed his fist on the desk. Rue didn't flinch, but squared herself and looked him straight in the eye.

"I don't need to answer to you or him," pointing at her and Noble individually. "And, I doubt that you're even old enough to vote."

"But I know plenty of people who are."

After a brief stare down between Rue and the official, he said, "You have two seconds to get out of my office!"

Noble pulled Rue out of the office and did not waste any time leaving the building.

"You just saw an example of the evil I just told you about back at the safe house. The nerve of that man, thinking that he could barter … what selfish, self-serving arrogance!"

Noble could tell by the tone of Rue's voice and the broken sentences that she was still pretty mad. *Somehow I need to get her to calm down.* Letting her vent a while longer, he said, "That was a very impressive performance in there. I thought you were going to punch the guy. Remind me never to get you mad at me."

Noble could see the tension leave Rue's face. A smile began to emerge. "I thought about it."

Once outside, they saw a park not far away where they could study their maps and decide on their next step.

While Rue arranged the maps on a picnic table, Noble thought about the encounter with the official.

"Why do you think the official was so interested in my clothes? Do you think he could have arranged a trade?

"I wouldn't trust him as far as I could throw him. If he would have got his hands on your clothes, you would have probably ended up just like your dad."

While Rue studied the maps, Noble walked around to the other side of the picnic table and sat down. He thought about Rue's response to his questions. *What's the mystery behind these clothes and what do they have to do with dad?* His mind wondered back to the lunch with his parents overlooking the beautiful valley and wondered how a nasty place like this could exist in such beauty.

As he sat staring at nothing, brightness caught his attention. He looked up to see if a cloud had opened in front of the sun, but he looked into a gray, overcast sky. He turned to Rue and asked, "Did you see that?"

She had stepped back from the table and was looking down. She pointed at the ground under the table and said, "This is another reason that the official was interested in your clothes."

He leaned to see to what she pointed. He saw a dark circle that surrounded the table. He jumped from the table and shouted, "What's that?" As he stepped away from the table, the circle moved with him.

"Rue?" He could actually see a shadow in this gloomy city.

Before she could respond, company arrived. About half dozen tormentors began making a wide circle around the table. They were not dressed like the ones Noble first encountered, but instead they were dressed in faded, multicolored suits. However, the expressions on their faces were the same: old and young at the same time, as though fear and anger had stolen their youth and happiness.

"Hey, pretty boy, your mama sure dresses you funny!" said one.

"Sure wish I had PJs like that. Do they come with matching diapers?" said another.

With his wide-eyed expression of awe, Noble would gaze at the dark circle, and then back at Rue, who had climbed over the table and was slowly backing toward him, watching the circling tormentors.

As she turned toward him to speak, one of the tormentors behind Noble said, "You should have gotten rid of your PJs when you had the chance!"

Out came the sword, and the chase was on. Noble struck the tormentor with the sword and yelled, "Take this back to your boss," referring to the official at the city building.

"*No!*" Rue yelled, but Noble kept going.

The tormentors scattered as Noble pursued, slashing with the sword. He appeared to be winning, but as the fiery darts began to fly, Rue was defenseless. Divide and conquer, one of the oldest tricks in the book, has caused even nations to fall. Unshielded, she was hit by a dart. Hearing her cry out in pain, he ran back and covered them both with the shield. Fiery darts filled the air as the tormentors once again circled them. Rue was hit again and screamed in pain. Dropping to the ground, Noble covered her as best he could. What Noble did not realize, and what Rue had not had a chance to explain to him at this point was the importance of the dark circle. As he covered Rue, the tormentors came closer, and the darts rang off the shield and pelted his clothes. When the battle appeared hopeless, Noble heard several screams coming from his attackers. He looked up to see flashes of light accompanied by screams as the tormentors came into contact with the dark circle. As a tormentor would prepare to throw a dart, the dark circle would counter by making contact with the tormentor. The battle ended with attackers retreating in smoldering, tattered suits.

"Tommy, do you understand how and why the tormentors were able to injure Rue?"

Tommy thought for a while. "I understand how, but I'm not sure why they wanted to hurt her. They were after him, right?"

"Yes, they were after him." Grandpa thought for a moment. "See if this helps. When Noble drew his sword and chased the tormentors, he went in anger and in his own strength, but still protected by his armored clothing. The evil tormentors, not really concerned who they hurt, were then able to throw their darts of fire at his defenseless companion. When he returned to Rue and covered her with the shield and himself, then the dark circle was able to surround both of them and come to their defense. Did that help any?"

"Oh. They couldn't hurt him so they hurt her. What's the dark circle? Where did it come from?"

"We'll get to that. Just be patient." Adjusting himself in the old stuffed chair, he continued.

Rue was hit in the shoulder close to her neck and in the side. The wounds looked horrible. He could tell that she was in a great deal of pain and near unconsciousness. Noble picked her up and began calling for help.

"Help me! Somebody please help!" He looked in every direction wondering what to do. The park was located in what looked like a business district. Quickly glancing around, seeing barred doors and windows on the buildings, he surmised that he would find more of what he encountered when he first entered the city called Peiratopos. *I have to get her back to the safe house. Or maybe someone in the city building will help us.*

Leaving the maps and Rue's shoulder bag on the table, Noble continued calling for help as he headed for the city building.

"Someone help us, please!" Looking at his injured friend, he said, "Hang on, Rue. Someone *will* help us in that building, or else."

"Wait!" a voice called from behind. Noble turned to see a woman motioning for him to come. "Bring her back to the table!"

Noble hurried to return back toward the picnic table. His arms cramped and the muscles in the small of his back burned from carrying Rue. Arching his back and running in a squatting gate, he pushed himself harder than ever. As he laid her as gently as he could on the table, the woman use Rue's bag as a pillow to support her neck.

"Thank you...so much...for helping," Noble said as he gasped for breath.

The woman examined Rue's wounds without responding to Noble. She opened a first aid kit and began cleaning the wound. Pulling fragments of dart and singed cloth from the wound, Rue jerked and rolled her head back and forth in her semi-conscious state.

"Hold her head still. This one looks serious. The one on her side's not quite as bad, but is still serious. When I finish bandaging this one, I need you to help me lift her so I can pull her shirt up past the wound on her side."

"Okay. Again, thank you for what you're doing."

"You're welcome. You're lucky that I was still in my office. I was just getting ready to leave when I saw some very upset tormentors run by. I found my first aid kit, ran out the door, and heard you calling."

As the woman finished bandaging the wound, Rue began moaning and regaining consciousness. Her eyes came wide open and she tried to set up.

"Easy girl. Just relax. You're okay. I need you to raise your hips up off the table. We'll help you. "

Rue pulled her feet up and raised her hips off the table. She gritted her teeth and groaned while the woman raised her shirt and began cleaning the wound. Noble held her hand and was near tears as he watched Rue try to lie still while the woman pulled pieces of dart and cloth out of the wound.

"Almost done. Lay as still as you can. One more piece and it appears to be pretty deep."

Rue closed her eyes tight and squeezed Nobles hand. He saw her jaw tighten and her body twitched when the woman began to dig for the last piece of dart.

"Got it. A little medicine and a bandage, and we're done. Relax."

Rue did just that. She stretched her legs out and let her middle relax. The tightness left her face. She let go of his hand to wipe tears from the corners of her eyes. He had to look away and deal with his own tears and the lump in his throat. The back of his hand burned where she had dug her nails, but he didn't care.

"Where are you guys staying?" the woman asked.

"We're from the Southern safe house," Rue answered.

"No way. That's too far. You're staying with me tonight. I have plenty of beds in my office and I'll stay with you. We're less than a block away. My name's Lillith, by the way. And you are?"

"I'm Noble. This is Rue."

"Noble, help Rue sit up. Let's see if she can walk. Hang on to her.

Rue took Noble's hand and pulled herself into a sitting position. The tightness in her jaw and the groaning returned as she slowly turned and set her feet on the table's bench seat. Noble waited in front of her until she was ready to step off the seat. She slowly turned and looked at the tabletop.

"Where are the maps?"

"The maps that were on the table are in the bag," Lillith replied.

Noble slipped Rue's bag over his shoulder and helped her off the table. The three moved slowly the short distance to Lillith's office.

Lillith's front office entry faced the north side of the city building. The street and sidewalk sloped downward between the buildings creating the need for five steps and a landing. Rue was not stepping up or down very well, so Lillith opted for the east side ground level entrance. Unlocking the door,

Lillith walked down a long hallway and waited in the office entry for Noble and Rue.

"Noble, at the end of this hallway there are two rooms with beds. Take Rue to the end room. I'm going to see if I can find Rue a happy pill that will help her sleep. I'll be down in a bit."

Noble and Rue entered a large room at the end of the hall. To their left, what appeared to be a closet with double sets of bypass doors covered most of the wall. To their right, a double bed with a sculptured headboard centered the north wall with nightstands on either side. Almost directly across from the door, a double window with sheer curtains offered light and a view of the building across the alley. On the east wall next to the door was a four-drawer dresser and an overstuffed chair.

"This is a big room for a bedroom," Rue observed.

Noble didn't respond. He directed Rue to the bed and helped her lay down. With a sigh of relief, she closed her eyes and relaxed.

He waited by the bed for a moment before moving to the window. Staring at the wall of the building across the alley, his mind was near overload from the events of the day. "What next?" he said aloud.

"Excuse me?" Noble jumped at the sound of Lillith's voice. "I'm sorry. I thought you were speaking to me."

"That's okay. I was talking to myself. It's been a crazy day."

Rue stirred at the sound of conversation. Lillith handed her a pill and a cup of water.

"This will help you sleep. You might feel a little pain, but you really won't care," Lillith grinned. "It's all I could find."

Rue examined the pill. "Ooh, I recognize this. Do you think I need something this strong?"

"Break it in half. If you wake up hurting, take the other half. It's up to you. You know how you feel." Lillith walked to the door. "I need to run an errand. I'll come check on you when I get back. I'm going to lock you in so you won't have to worry about intruders. There's a bed in the next room, Noble, and the restroom's right down the hall." She turned and moved quickly down the hall.

Noble watched her until she disappeared into a room past the entryway. He continued to stare, his mind returning to the events of the day.

"She's very pretty, isn't she?"

"Huh?" Noble heard her speak, but what she said didn't register.

"I said, she's very pretty, isn't she?"

"Oh. I suppose. I hadn't really noticed." He continued to stare down the hall.

"Okay," Rue laughed softly. "Come over here and tell me another big lie."

Noble turned toward her to see a big smile on her face. He returned the smile and slowly walked to the chair and sat down. She watched him sit quietly with his head down.

"Are you okay?" she asked.

"Yes and no," he choked, and continued looking at the floor.

Realizing his injury was not physical, she asked, "What kind of answer's that?" trying to lighten the moment.

43

"I'm not wounded on the outside, but my anger nearly got you killed," he replied choking back tears, "and this is how I repay your kindness.

"Well, great warrior, just don't let it happen again," Rue laughed. Still smiling, she turned her head and closed her eyes.

Noble began to think about everything that had happened as Rue drifted off to sleep. His father, the city, the armor, Rue—this is no accident.

"How is she?" came a quiet voice, snapping him from his thought and raising him out of his chair like an electric shock. "Sorry. Still a little jumpy, I see." Lillith walked to the foot of the bed. "Is she sleeping?"

"Yes. She drifted off right after you left."

"Come, let her rest. Let's sit out here and talk. It will take your mind off of things." She reached for his hand and led him out of the room and down the hall.

The room that they entered had a long, narrow table and thick-padded chairs lined each side. There were shelves on the walls with all sorts of statues and shadow boxes filled with figures. Any voids were filled with pictures. Some were strange but interesting. Before he could look closely at his surroundings, the woman asked, "Are you hungry?"

"What?" Noble jumped again.

"Are you sure you're okay? You don't act like you're with me." The woman looked concerned as she pulled a chair from the table for him.

"I'm okay. It's just, well, a lot has happened." He sat down.

She put her hands on his shoulders and began a massage that relieved his tension down to his toes. She then asked again, "Are you hungry?"

"Yes, I believe I am. I don't know how long it's been since I've eaten," he responded in a very relaxed voice.

"You didn't jump," she said jokingly. "What would you like to eat?"

"Whatever you have I'm sure will be fine." He rolled his head in a circle. "Thank you," he said in response to the massage.

The woman brought out a meat tray with cheese, crackers, and different kinds of bread. She then returned with a pitcher of water and some kind of mixed fruit drink. While she was out of the room, Noble managed a closer look at the pictures and figures, but most of his thoughts were on Rue.

As they ate together, the woman intently asked about his visit to the city, how he met Rue, and his unusual clothes, all mixed with casual conversation. When the conversation got to the battle and Rue's wounds, he realized what the woman had said when she came to their aid.

"You said that you saw the tormentors and went to find your first aid kit. How did you know that we would need help?"

"Oh," she said smiling, "you're not the first to come through the city dressed like that."

"How many others? When?" he asked with excitement.

"Not many and it's been a while," she assured, trying to play down his excitement.

"When? Today, yesterday, last week, when?" Noble hoped it would be a lead on his father.

"Oh! No. It's been a year or two since I heard of the last Shadow Walker," she said while filling his glass.

"Shadow Walker? Is that what I'm called?" He saw surprise in the woman's expression.

"Yes. That's what you're called here." She tried to cover her surprise that he did not recognize the name.

Why didn't Rue mention this name? What did it mean? he thought. Some of his conversation with the official at the city building began to make sense. They sat quietly for a while and finished eating.

Lillith cleared the table and said, "I'm going to check on your friend."

"Yes. I think I will come along as well."

Rue was sleeping soundly as they looked in on her. He motioned that he would sleep in the chair and she agreed. Her room was the next room down the hallway if needed. He waited for her to leave the room before taking his seat. She stopped at the door, turned and gave him a scrutinizing stare. She finally smiled and reached out her hand. Noble returned the smile, took her hand, and softly said, "Thank you for all that you have done. Good night."

LILLITH

CHAPTER 5

Rue slept through the night and was the first to awake when light entered the window. She could not decide what hurt more, her wounds or hunger. When she sat up in the bed, her stirring woke Noble.

"Good morning, great warrior," she said with that same little smile.

"How do you feel, Rue?"

"I'm hungry. Did you eat anything last night?" She tried to stretch, but changed her mind.

"Yes," he replied, watching her, trying not to act sore.

"Well! Thanks for inviting me. Just drug me up, dump me in a bed, and go have dinner with a beauty," Rue pouted, acting put out like when he first discovered his armor.

"You were sound asleep. Do you always wake up so cheerful?" Noble poked, beginning to appreciate her personality.

"Only when I've been shot." She looked at him with that same little smile.

He smiled back and thought about how fortunate he was to have met her. He could not think of anyone that he had become so close to so quickly. He would never leave her unprotected again.

"How's our patient?" Lillith asked as she breezed into the room.

"Grumpy," Noble said, still smiling at Rue.

"That's a good sign. Hungry?" Lillith asked, directing her attention toward Rue.

"Yes!"

"That's even a better sign. Come on Noble, let's get Rue some breakfast."

Noble pushed himself out of the chair, stretched, and stumbled toward the door. He followed Lillith down the hall to where she stopped, opened the bathroom door, and made a quick look. She then returned to the bedroom.

"Just in case you don't remember from last night, the bathroom's right down the hall, Rue. Otherwise, stay put and rest. We'll be right back." She then returned, breezed past Noble, and said, "Had to make a TP check."

Rue now wondered what hurt her more: her wounds, her hunger, or the woman's beauty. Surely Noble had noticed. She had never been jealous that she could recall. She had just met Noble. They barely had time to be friends. Why did she feel this way about Lillith?

"How dumb," she said aloud as she reminded herself about Lillith's help. "She may have saved my life, or at least saved me from a bad infection." She eased out of bed and made her way to the restroom. When she returned to her room, she sat on the side of the bed and continued to wonder about Lillith.

Breakfast finally arrived, and Rue was famished. A bed tray was placed across her lap. A large bowl of warm oats, a jar of honey, some fresh fruit, toast, bacon and eggs, all served from a fold-up table placed next to the bed. They all ate in the bedroom and talked. Actually, Lillith did most of the talking. Their hostess was quite a conversationalist.

"Well, you need some rest. Noble, would you help me clean up, please?" Lillith began stacking plates on a serving tray.

"Yes, I would." He reached for the tray.

"The maps! Did you get the maps?" Rue asked in a panic.

Noble gave Rue a puzzled look. "Yes, Lillith put them in your shoulder bag. You don't remember, do you? They're okay," he assured her.

Rue thought for a moment. "Oh. Yes. I do remember. Thank you, Lillith. I wouldn't want to see our friend again."

"Me either. He wasn't too happy with us when we left the city building. I'd say that he was behind our visitors in the park, since they knew about his offer."

"I see that you have met our mayor," said Lillith.

"How did you know who we were talking about?" they asked almost word for word.

Lillith placed the last of the dishes on her tray and headed down the hallway, ignoring the question.

Noble folded the portable table, picked up the remaining trays, and started to follow Lillith.

"Wow," Rue said, "I almost punched the mayor."

Noble stopped and looked at her. She sat on the side of the bed staring thoughtfully toward the chair where he slept. She slowly turned and looked at him and smiled. *Wow, indeed,* he thought. He couldn't help but return the smile and shake his head in disbelief and amazement.

When he started to leave, Rue said, "Hey. Where's my bag?"

"Top dresser drawer."

"I'm going to freshen up and get out the maps. Come back after you help Lillith."

"You need to rest."

"I'm okay. I heal quickly."

"Right. I saw those wounds. I don't think they're going to heal too quickly. Rest," he said.

As he started to leave the room again, the look he got from Rue delivered the message, *don't be gone long!*

"Okay, I'll be back as soon as I can."

He helped Lillith clean up the kitchen and returned to Rue. She sat in the middle of the bed with her legs crossed, and with the maps spread semi-circle around her. She signaled with her finger to her lips for him to be quiet.

"What?" he asked in a soft but firm voice as he entered the room.

She motioned for him to push the door closed and to come closer to the bed. "I don't trust her," she replied, mouthing the words in a whisper. "She's too nice."

"Too nice? What kind of reason is that for not trusting her? She's feeding us, giving us a place to stay, and letting you heal. I don't understand."

"That's what I mean. She's *too* nice," Rue replied still whispering. "I have never met anyone outside my group that nice."

"Do you mean to tell me that you and your group are the only nice people in this city? How many people have you met outside your group?" Noble asked, trying to defend Lillith a little.

"Well, not very many. But you would think that out of my group that they would know some nice people from the city and tell the rest of us about them. She just doesn't fit in with the tormentors or the current city inhabitants. She's just too … perfect."

"How often do you go into the city?" He continued his line of questions with a target in mind.

"No more often than we need to. It's not very pleasant with the tormentors lurking about."

"I can understand that," he agreed. "While we're being candid, tell me about the Shadow Walkers."

A look came over Rue's face that took him back a bit. A surprised but joyful look that was so radiant, you would have thought that her wounds had been instantly healed.

"You saw it!" Rue exclaimed, almost leaping out of bed.

"Saw what?" Noble stepped back and braced himself, expecting her to leap on him at any time.

"You didn't see it." She eased back down on the bed, being reminded of her wounds by the quick movement.

"See what? Tell me what I was supposed to see and I will tell you if I saw it or not," he asked very slowly, overemphasizing every word.

"The dark circle, your shadow," Rue said mockingly with her little smile.

"I saw the dark circle you pointed to while we were looking at the maps. But, the sky was overcast, so how could that have been my shadow?"

"That's true. The sky was overcast. It wasn't "your" shadow."

"Well, whose shadow was it then? Yours? You were on the other side of the table," he snapped facetiously.

"Well, it was your shadow and it wasn't." Rue smiled, knowing that this would get him going.

"Great! Now we're getting somewhere. Do you need more drugs before you explain yourself?" He turned as if to leave the room.

"Wait." She moved suddenly and again was reminded of her wounds. She eased back down on the bed. "Sit, let me tell you what I have heard."

"What you have heard?"

"Please, sit." She patted the side of the bed next to the chair where he had spent the night. Her expression was still joyful and radiant in spite of her pain. Noble was not really going to leave the room. As a matter of fact, if his father walked through the door right now, he would be torn between embracing him or listening to Rue.

She explained that the citizens who reported seeing visitors dressed like him also told of a shadow that went before them, no matter where the sun was located in the sky. There were different stories as to what the shadow did, but all that came into the city dressed like Noble came with a shadow.

"What were some of the things they say that the shadow did?" he asked.

"Some say that it's a guide, others say it's for protection, but all agree that those who walk in the shadow are never to get in front of it."

"They're both right," Lillith said as she appeared in the room like a ghost. Neither of them saw or heard her enter. Maybe they were just too engrossed in their conversation— or were they?

"And there's more," Lillith added, directing her attention towards Noble. "I can teach you to use the shadow. Together we can find your father and rule this city. You would be doing everyone a great service by ridding the city of tormentors. Families will be able to return to their homes. Business will reopen. With the tormentors gone, children will play in the streets again. Others like yourself that enter the city will be treated kindly and not be in danger of the darts that caused your friend's wounds. If you want my help, I will be in the conference room. What I have to say is for your ears only."

During her speech, Lillith never took her eyes off Noble. She did not look him in the eyes exactly; it was as if she was trying to get inside him. When finished speaking, she continued to gaze in silence, and moved slowly to the door.

When she had left the room, they both sat silently for a moment. When Noble stood to leave the room, Rue touched his arm. He jumped a little, as though he had forgotten that she was there. He turned toward her, and she whispered the same words as before: "I don't trust her." Noble nodded with an expressionless look on his face, turned, and headed for the door.

Lillith waited with arms folded, facing the wall on the opposite side of the room. She turned as she heard him enter. *She was more beautiful than ever*, he thought. Or maybe it's the moment. What was he about to hear? Would he understand any of it? He could not even remember walking down the hall. They both stood motionless, facing each other. Finally, she smiled and motioned for him to be seated.

"You have no idea what you have, do you?" He offered no answer. Lillith was looking at him as before, as though trying to search his mind. She began moving slowly around the table as she talked.

"Before I explain the power you have, and begin to teach you to use it, you must agree to these conditions. Because of the danger involved in cleaning up the city, Rue must return home where she will be safe. As payment for what I'm about to do, I will rule this city at your side." She leaned down from behind him and whispered in his ear, "You will make a great king, and your queen will be very grateful." She continued slowly around the table, watching him the whole time. He sat expressionless and motionless for a moment, looking straight ahead. His thoughts were scrambled as images raced through his mind. The thought that brought him back into focus was Rue's safety. He finally looked at Lillith and began to speak. Her beauty almost hurt his eyes.

"Rue's safety makes sense. I need to speak to her for a moment. Please excuse me." Noble pushed back from the table. His legs felt like rubber as he walked down the hallway. He paused several times trying to think of what he would say to Rue. He finally entered the room but still did not know what to say.

She was sitting on the edge of the bed with her back to the door. She turned, looked him straight in the eye, and said, "You're going with her, aren't you?"

Still speechless, and with a blank expression on his face, Noble moved slowly to the chair and sat down. He finally spoke. "I almost got you killed. Why should you continue to put yourself in danger? You should return home as Lillith has suggested."

"Is this what you want me to do?" She moved over beside him.

"It's best." Unable to look at the hurt on her face, he turned toward the floor. She was now in front of him on one knee, again staring intently into his eyes.

"Is this what "you" want?"

"Not really." Noble finally expressed himself without Lillith's manipulative words.

Her expression changed from hurt to that little smile that he would have really missed, and then said, "Then let's go find your dad."

"What did you say? Oh, yes. My dad." His mind was still swimming a little. Rue took his hand and turned toward the door. Lillith was in the room just as mysteriously as before.

"You should return home." Lillith's tone was firm and commanding.

"I will do as Noble wishes," Rue replied in the same tone.

"He wishes you to return home." Lillith now turned her focus on Noble.

"He didn't say that to me." Rue boldly moved between Lillith and Noble in an effort to distract her and give him a chance to answer.

"What do you say, my king? Your queen awaits an answer." Lillith ignored Rue's move, focusing her comments on his confused mind.

Noble finally came to his senses. Rue was right. *I came here looking for my dad, not a kingdom or a queen,* he thought. He was now able to look past Lillith's beauty and enticing words and into her eyes. They were empty, like the tormentors. As soon as he made eye contact, she looked towards Rue as if to speak to her. Noble placed his hand on the sword, to make ready a defense if necessary. It was at that same moment, a message from within said, *Resist and stand firm in the evil day.*

"You just want my armor and what it can do for you," Noble heard himself say. What they saw next went beyond imagination. An uncontrollable rage came over Lillith. Before she could leave the room, her face began to show her true nature. She had used the witchcraft of deceitful words and seemingly kind deeds to gain their trust and the use of Noble's gifts. As she began to speak, unintelligible words came out as flaming darts. She was a tormentor.

Noble managed to get the shield in front of Rue in time, but before he could draw the sword, the shadow went before them. With a sizzling flash, Lillith screamed and ran out of the room. Seconds later, they heard the slamming of a door, and then silence. Again, Noble made a profound statement. "Wow!" Rue was speechless.

Captured motionless, the "great warrior" and his wounded companion gazed toward the empty doorway. Four walls that just moments before echoed pointed conversation was now thick with silence. Noble's voice finally broke the stillness.

"I saw it," he said.

"Saw what?" she asked, still dazed.

"In the park; I saw the shadow do the same thing to the tormentors," Noble said as he turned Rue around to face him. Rue finally understood what he was saying. That radiant, joyful look came over her again. Her eyes were full of fire and wonder. Her smile was so beautiful he thought that he heard laughter. He could see her body shaking with excitement.

"Let's go find your dad."

Even her voice sounded different, but her words brought him back to the purpose before them. Gathering the maps and their gear, the travelers carefully checked the house before they let their guard down. It was empty. The large table in the conference room was the perfect place to study the maps. Rue arranged the maps while Noble watched for intruders. She wrote notes on the areas that she had visited before. She listed who she thought controlled the area and where they might be found. Noble realized what she was doing and emotion came over him again.

"Why are you marking the maps?" he asked, knowing the answer.

"In case we get separated."

"Or in case I get you killed," Noble replied in a choked voice. Rue realized the seriousness of the situation and understood his concern. However, she eased the moment with some levity. Shaking her fist at him, she smiled and said, "If you keep talking like that, I'll show you what your shadow won't protect you from."

Noble gave her a little grin, but Rue could tell that he was troubled, so with a more serious look, she walked to the door where he stood watch, her eyes still glistening like fire as she looked in his, and said, "This is my choice. If I don't make it, you're to continue on, find your dad, and then use the maps to get back to the safe house. They can guide you to the path at the edge of the city."

"I thought you said that it was useless trying to escape, that the tormentors would only bring you back."

"That was before I knew for sure that you would be a shadow walker. They will more than likely be glad when you leave," she explained and moved back to the table.

"Are you keeping something from me again?" he asked with a little sarcasm.

"I have told you all that I know. I have heard the others say that the tormentors hate the shadow, so I reasoned that they would be glad to see you go." When she leaned over the table and stretched her arms, Noble saw her jerk.

"Let me see your wounds," he said as he left his post.

"They're fine." She got a look that said he was not going to take no for an answer. "Okay, here. Look and see. I told you that I heal quickly." She raised her shirt and bandage. "Wow. You weren't kidding. That looks much better. But, that's a deep puncture wound. And the other is so close to your neck. You really should go back to the safe house and get them cared for," he said with concern.

"You will miss me." He got the grin with her fiery eyes. He could not argue with that. Her character had helped him overcome his fears and self-doubt. With a more serious look she added, "Besides, now we both have seen what protection the shadow gives us. And if you run off and leave me again, you better hope they kill me this time," she said, shaking her fist at him again.

"Okay," he said with a smile. "But you better keep up." He turned and marched out the door.

"Hey!" She quickly gathered the maps and hurried after him. He had stepped to the side just outside the door. When she came through, she almost ran into him. They both laughed. Noble had never had a friend like this one.

"How do you like the story so far?" Grandpa thought he could see his reflection in Tommy's glassy-eyed stare. "We better get some sleep if we're going to be up before the fish."

"'Night, Grandpa." Tommy crawled into his sleeping bag and was asleep when his head hit the pillow. A blessed old man sat for a moment reflecting on the day just spent with this great young man. He quietly left the chair and banked the fire. Before turning in, he took one more look at the scene at the other end of the cabin. Shadows of flickering firelight danced on a sleeping boy and an old dog. The only sounds that break the silence are night creatures, a crackling fire, and the restful breathing of a boy and a dog.

MARION DAVID RUSSELL

IN HIS SHADOW

CHAPTER 6

In what seemed like only moments, Tommy awoke to the smell of bacon.

"Hey, sleepyhead. Rise and shine."

"What time is it?" Tommy sat up and stretched.

"6 a.m." Tommy fell back on the cot and let out a loud moan.

"Hehe. Come on now. Get up, get your duds on and eat. We've got a big day ahead of us," Grandpa coaxed. "Ol' Butch is even ready." The dog was lying close to the cook just in case he dropped something.

With breakfast finished and cleaned up, they headed down the path to the dock. The morning air was crisp and clean. New songs had now replaced the music of the night.

Light of sunrise exposed details of color and beauty to the silhouettes of the previous evening.

"Come on, Butch," Tommy called. Butch ambled over to the corner of the porch and lay down in the morning sun.

"He isn't much of a fisherman, but I'll bet he'll help us eat some," Grandpa said with a chuckle.

Once past the trees, the path brought the fishermen to a wooden dock. Grandpa stopped for a moment. The view was magnificent. The morning sun had just started to rise over the green hill to the east. The brightness almost hurt their eyes. A fine mist was rising from the lake to meet the sun's rays racing over the hill.

"Wow. You just can't get a view like this in the city," marveled Grandpa.

"This almost makes getting up early worth it. Let's catch some fish," Tommy said mockingly. The old man grabbed Tommy and pretended like he was going to throw him in the lake. They loaded their gear into the boat and headed for their first stop. They had just put their lines in the water when the shadow of a large bird slowly floated across them.

"Neat shadow, huh, Grandpa?" Can you tell me some more of the story about the shadow? I don't think I can wait till tonight."

"You like the story, do you? Well, let's see. Where did we leave off?"

"They were just leaving that evil lady's house," prompted Tommy.

"Lillith's?"

"Yeah, her."

"Okay."

When the travelers left Lillith's office, they walked into the street between the city building and her front entrance. Rue began describing a systematic plan to cover the city. While listening to Rue, Noble scanned the area, watching for unwelcome company. He noticed something about the front of Lillith's building that he did not notice the previous evening. Calling Rue's attention to the object, he interrupted her and said, "Will you look at that?" Rue turned and saw the sign hanging over the front entrance.

LILLITH's
Palm Reading
Fortune-telling

"We had better pay more attention to the company we keep," she said.

"And to the buildings we enter," he added. "I didn't see that sign last night."

Focusing their attention again on the maps, they heard familiar voices approaching from behind. They turned to see some of their previous attackers emerge from exterior stairs leading from the basement of the city building.

"Well, look here guys, she's still alive. At least we found out who the tough one is," one said.

"Yeah, she didn't turn and run like PJ boy did," said another. The tormentors began to circle the travelers.

"I'll bet she had to change his diapers after our last meeting." The hideous laughing and sneers were coming from all around them.

"Come on, pretty boy, I'll bet you can't catch me."

Before the tormentors even began to circle, Noble had the shield ready and his hand on the sword. Rue wedged herself between him and the shield before the darts began to fly. Unlike before, the darts now came from every direction, and the tormentor's attack was more aggressive. This time Noble listened to the inner voice without hesitation, and the shadow went before them even stronger.

Resist and stand firm in the evil day, the inner voice said as the darts of fire sizzled through the air. The tormentors' laughter became screams of pain when touched by the shadow. The battle came swiftly to an end with the tormentors in retreat.

"Are you okay?" Noble asked.

"Never better." Rue peeked out from behind the shield. Noble turned to look behind them.

"Did you feel the darts that hit you in the back?" Rue asked.

"No." Noble turned to look over his shoulder. They both looked on the ground around them. There were smoldering pieces of dart laying everywhere.

Noble removed the shield from his hand and latched it over his shoulder. "I saw something that you might be interested in. You might have seen it, too, if you hadn't buried your face in my chest. The darts that would have hit your legs, the back of your head, or my face were drawn to the shield."

"I'm sticking to you like glue, pal," she said with that famous grin. She put her arm around his waist and slipped her fingers under his belt. As they began to move forward, he put his arm around her shoulder and gently pulled her close. He was not smiling.

"Stay close. I think these guys are serious." Keeping a watchful eye on their surroundings, they moved with a firm pace into the afternoon without any visitors.

Entering the first part of the city that Rue had marked on the map, Noble commented that the shadow had become more egg-shaped.

"Speaking of eggs," she said, "I'm getting hungry."

"Me too. Should I assume that you have no fast food places here?"

"And what would you pay for it with, O Rich One?" she teased.

"I might trade you for a large cheeseburger, O Thorn-In-My-Side." She tried to push away from him, but he held her tight. "You're not going anywhere. I can't read the maps and watch for visitors at the same time. Besides, every time I look at the maps, we get attacked. I'm not looking at them anymore. That's your job." They looked at one another and smiled.

They came to the end of the street. They needed to decide which way to turn. Rue looked at the map of that area, but had no idea in what direction to go.

"Well, pick one," he said.

"I'm following you."

"Chicken," he teased.

"In case you haven't noticed, genius, we're both in the egg," she replied with witty sarcasm.

"But you're here by choice. Not too smart, are you? You could be home eating a big sandwich right now," he said, returning the sarcasm. He really enjoyed her wit.

"Thanks for reminding me," she said as she rubbed her belly. "At least it's not a forced diet."

"Let's go this way," he said, finally deciding. But when they turned and took a few steps, the egg-shaped end of the shadow pointed in the opposite direction. They stopped and looked at each other.

Rue broke the silence. "Did you see that?"

Still staring at her he said, "Let's go the other way."

"Good thinking," she replied as they turned in the direction of the long end of the shadow and proceeded.

The looks of the city had not changed much. The same mixture of buildings he first saw when he entered Peiratopos lined the streets of this section. According to the maps, they headed west when they left Lillith's. The area that they passed through before turning north was more residential. Bars on the doors and windows and still no one moving about: *back home there would be total strangers waving from their porches*. The barred doors and windows reminded him of a jail. *What a horrible place to have to live*, he thought. It was not long until they saw why the shadow had turned in this direction. Up ahead was a house that looked like the one where he had met Rue.

"How about that?" said Noble.

"Are you still going to trade me for a cheeseburger?" she asked.

"With pickles?" This time she did not pull away but gave him a good elbow in the side, which he felt.

"You're getting real close to experiencing what the shadow won't protect you from, buddy," she warned with her grin. Then she slipped her arm around his waist and said, "I can't think of any place that I'd rather be."

When the people in the house saw the travelers coming, they went out to greet them and invited them in. As Noble entered the house, another marvelous event took place. The shadow surrounded the house. Noble again waxed eloquently: "Wow!" But Rue was off looking for food and did not see the phenomenon.

That evening, they rested and visited with their hosts. They tried not talking about the events of the day, but conversation would eventually return to their journey. They did not get many visitors like Noble at the safe house, so naturally they would have many questions.

This particular safe house had a large closed in porch. Casement windows ran the length of one outside wall, resting on a three-foot knee wall covered with knotty pine. The exterior entrance had double doors with half glass and triple casement windows on either side. Decorative wood pocket doors gave access from the dining room.

Noble relaxed in a big comfortable chair and, naturally, was the center of attention. Every seat in the room was filled, and some of the younger ones sat on the floor.

"Can we see your sword?" one of the younger ones asked.

Noble pulled out the short sword and held it for all the younger ones to see. Though not much bigger than a large dagger, it was very ornate with all sorts of markings on the blade and handle. As Noble held the sword and turned it, light danced from the burnished blade.

"Wow! How many tormentors have you killed with it?" the same one asked.

Noble laughed. "None. I tried, but that didn't work out too well, did it, Rue?

"No, it didn't, great warrior," Rue grinned.

"Where did you get your clothes?" another of the younger ones asked.

"That's a good question," Noble squirmed.

"Yah, Noble, tell them about your clothes," Rue laughed.

"Thanks for your help, Rue. Why don't you tell them about my clothes?"

"I'd be glad to," Rue grinned. "Would you believe that he doesn't know where he got his clothes?"

The room burst with laughter. Noble blushed a little, but joined right in with the laughter.

"Rue, tell them about meeting the mayor," Noble grinned.

"No. You go ahead. I embarrassed you, now you can embarrass me. That's only fair."

"We went to the city building to get a map of the city. Different individuals questioned us before we were given our map. Finally, we end up in the mayor's office, but we didn't know that he was the mayor. Rue didn't like the way he was talking to us, so she got in his face and was ready to punch him. She got us thrown out of the city building."

Everyone laughed as Rue stood up and took a bow.

Rue stayed close to Noble and let him do most of the talking. She reasoned that it was his quest and that he should say or not say what he wanted them to know. He did not really mind talking about it. He was just tired. He had been wound pretty tight since Rue's injury, and it sure felt good to relax without fear of attack. Rue had her wounds dressed, and they looked much better. She had not stopped eating all evening. Noble began teasing her, saying, "You had better be able to walk tomorrow. As much as you're eating, I won't be able to carry you." She gave it right back about the shadow not protecting him from her. They laughed and enjoyed the moment.

Once some of the younger ones headed for bed, Noble asked about his father.

"Has any of you seen or heard of another stranger in town? Rue believes that the tormentors have captured my dad."

Onan, the overseer of the safe house answered, "You and Rue are the first visitors we have had in a long time. The city's so dangerous and almost everyone has left or moved into a safe house. I'm sorry to say that no one has seen or heard anything about your father."

"Tell me about the safe houses. Why does Kuriopolis allow them to exist?" Noble asked.

"We believe that the Higher Powers protect us, just as your shadow protects you," Onan replied.

"Are there more safe houses in the city," Rue asked.

"Yes," Onan nodded. "There's at least one in every section of the city. I will mark your maps with their general locations."

"Yes. Please do," Rue said excitedly, as she and Onan left the room to retrieve the maps from her shoulder bag.

Once Rue left the room, Noble addressed the remaining residence in a more serious tone. Drawing the sword again, he said, "One of the younger ones asked me earlier about this sword. It appears that this isn't a weapon for attacking or killing, although it's sharp and could be used for that. What I'm about to tell you may sound strange; it sounds strange to me, but it has happened three times now, the first time by accident.

When the mayor in the city building questioned Rue and me, the handle of the sword became caught under the arm of the chair I was sitting in. When gripping the handle to free it, the answer to the mayor's question came to me. I heard myself say in response to his offer for my clothes, "The clothes are a gift and not a bartering chip." I had never thought of the clothes as a gift before I heard myself say that."

"The next two times were the same message. When I placed my hand on the sword, I heard: Resist and stand firm in the evil day. These messages came when confronted by Lillith in her office, and then by a group of tormentors at the rear of the city building." Noble returned the sword to its sheath. "When I used the sword to attack the first group of tormentors Rue and I encountered, I nearly got her killed. It seems that this sword has a defensive purpose rather than offensive."

Noble received more questions about the sword and the rest of his armor from the group that remained. He didn't have a lot of answers, but did the best he could. As the evening grew long, the residence politely excused themselves, seeing that their guest was worn out. When Rue returned to the room, Noble was alone and nearly asleep in the chair.

"Come on, sleepy head. Our rooms are ready."

After a good night's sleep and a good breakfast, Noble and Rue left the house with a blessing and food supply for the day. A place to sleep and some food was plenty of help as the travelers began another day in the city.

The morning travel passed the same way as the day before, with one exception. About two or three blocks on either side, they could see the little robed beings scurrying about. With no change in the scenery, the activity in the distance, while a bit unnerving, was at least entertaining. Around noon, they stopped to eat and rest.

"Why have we not been attacked again?" Noble wondered.

"The news of the whipping the shadow gave them yesterday may have spread through the city rather quickly," Rue suggested.

"Maybe. Back home, news traveled pretty fast when anything unusual happened." His thought had been on home all morning. He wondered what his mother was going through. *Did the police come and give her any help? Did they know about this place? Did she find the path and the door? Or worse, had she entered the city to look for them?* He tried to keep his thoughts on Rue's safety and finding his father. But the longer he sat, the more distracted he became.

"Come on," Rue said. "We better get moving." She could tell he was troubled. She tried making light conversations, but he was half listening.

"Wake up and stay with me," she said in a firm voice.

"What do you want?"

"You seem distracted. Talk to me. Tell me what's on your mind," she almost demanded.

"Just thinking of home, wondering what Mom's going through."

"Nothing you can do about it," she said pointedly.

"That's a little cold-hearted, isn't it?" He went from distracted to irked. For the first time, he was about to lose his temper with her.

"Maybe," she said. "But if your mind's there and your body's here, you may not be ready for what's up ahead." As she was speaking, a figure came out of a side street three blocks ahead and walked toward them. They could hardly believe their eyes. The armor was very familiar as well as the shield. Could it be? The person came close enough to call to them. No, it was not his father. The voice was female.

"It's good to see a friendly face!" she called.

"Should we trust this?" Rue whispered.

"I don't know. I sure want to. We could use the company and the help," he said as he pulled her close.

"Gee, thanks," Rue said, keeping her sharp wit even in the face of potential danger.

"You know what I mean." He didn't check for the grin, however. His attention was fixed on the woman.

"Where're you headed?" asked the woman.

"Not sure," Noble replied. "We're looking for someone."

"Did you come from that direction?" The woman stopped about a half block away and pointed behind them.

"Yes"

"Well, I came from back there. Tell me who you're looking for. Maybe I saw him." She turned slightly and pointed behind her. She was carrying her shield in front of her and standing in the shadow of a building, but Rue's sharp eye picked up something strange.

"How did you know it was a man?" he asked while Rue was trying to get his attention.

"Lucky guess." The woman paused, and then added, "Just a figure of speech."

"Why doesn't she have a belt on?" Rue whispered. "When she turned, I didn't see a belt like yours."

"Who's your friend?" the woman asked, keeping the conversation flowing. She and Rue spoke at the same time so he did not hear what Rue said.

He raised his hand toward the woman and said, "Excuse me just a moment." Turning to Rue but keeping his eye on the woman, he asked, "What did you say?"

"She doesn't have a belt on."

"She doesn't have a helmet on, either," he returned. "So keep your eyes open and stay close."

"Don't worry."

"I'm sorry. What did you ask?" Noble said to the woman.

"Who's your friend?"

"Someone I met at a safe house who has agreed to guide me through the city," he explained.

"Is that a bandage I see? Is she injured?"

"You need to answer some of my questions before I answer any more of yours. Where are your helmet and your belt?"

"Since you're not going to answer any more of my questions, I'll assume that I'm the first female Shadow Walker that you have met." She then waited for him to respond.

"You didn't answer my question. Come closer," he requested.

"Why should I trust you any more than you trust me?"

"This isn't a very nice place," he said, "full of surprises."

"Yes, I know," the woman agreed. "That's why I prefer to keep my distance for now.

"Well, we can't stand here all day not trusting each other," he pointed out, "so we're coming to you."

"Are you crazy?" Rue whispered assertively.

"If she's a shadow walker and sees our shadow, why should she fear us? Stay close and keep those fiery eyes peeled." They moved closer to the woman until they could see her face. She was very nervous. Her eyes were darting from side to side as if she expected someone or maybe a trap. Noble pulled his shield from his shoulder and made ready a defense.

"We're not going to hurt you," Noble assured the woman. "How could we, anyway? Your shadow will protect you."

"That's close enough," she said trying to be forceful, but her voice and eyes had fear in them. He did not stop. The buildings shadow vanished when his shadow touched it.

"Stop!" The woman shrieked in a loud and fearful voice.

"Where's your shadow?" Noble demanded.

"Stop, please, stop! I don't know what will happen if I step into the shadow again," she said almost in tears. Noble stopped. His hand now on the sword instinctively, listening for any sign of deception, as well as a message from within.

He's learning to use his gifts well, Rue thought. Delighted, however, she was not smiling but preoccupied at the moment, watching the woman and the area around them.

"Go on," he said.

"I have finished my mission and am trying to find my way out of the city." Her voice was still shaking. Rue nudged him with her elbow and he glanced at her and nodded.

"If you have been to a safe house, you should know the way out. I haven't completed my mission yet, and I know to go to a safe house when finished." The woman did not answer. "Where's your helmet, belt, and shadow?" he asked when she did not respond.

"Ask her about Lillith." A male voice came from behind them. The woman closed her eyes and literally shook in her boots. Noble thought that Rue had jumped inside his armor. However, he stood like a stone, his eyes fixed on the woman.

"Come around in front of me where I can see you and the woman," Noble said in a calm but uncompromising voice. The man did as he was asked, bowed, and introduced himself.

"My name's Hanani. I'm the prophet of the city. This pitiful beast I call Esau because she sold her belt of truth to Lillith and therefore lost her helmet of salvation and her inheritance of the shadow. She now works for me, checking out visitors in this section. I apologize to you, young lady, for frightening you that way. We can't be too careful when it comes to strangers."

"I'm okay," Rue said, but still quite shaken.

"Some lookout you are," Noble said out of the side of his mouth. "I should've brought the cheeseburger for a lookout," he added, trying to lighten the moment and calm her down. He didn't see the look he got from her because he was watching the two in front of them. It would have been as devastating as the fiery darts had he been outside the protection of the shadow. But it worked. She was the old Rue again.

"That can be arranged at the next safe house," she clarified softly.

"Welcome back," he uttered with a little grin. At the same time that they were exchanging their under-the-breath abuses, Hanani dismissed the woman who gladly turned and hurried off.

"That could have been me," Noble said, feeling compassion for the woman.

"Yes, it could have," Rue replied, now in a solemn tone.

Hanani, now turning his attention back to the travelers said, "Well, my new friends, how can I assist you on your journey?"

"Pardon us if we don't seem too trusting," Rue said with a look that only she could give. This produced a hearty laugh from Hanani, who again apologized.

"Yes, I did give you quite a start. Please, again forgive me," he said, trying to be sincere. Rue glanced at Noble, who was biting his lip and watching her out of the corner of his eye. This got him another good elbow, which triggered another good laugh from the prophet.

"I probably won't live this down," Rue said. This broke Noble's tension. He dropped his shield a little and laughed out loud. Laughter is contagious. Even Rue joined in.

MARION DAVID RUSSELL

THE PROPHET

CHAPTER 7

There was truth in what Rue said about trust. While they followed Hanani to his residence, she told Noble that she had never heard of a "prophet of the city" mentioned at the safe house, but she admitted that she had not heard that all sections of the city had safe houses either. However, they agreed that they had a few more questions that needed answers before they would trust the prophet's help.

Hanani's residence was in a building much like the city building where they went for maps. The inside, however, looked more like a theater than a public office building. When they asked about it, he gave them quite a history of the building. In short, it was built at a time when the arts thrived in the city. It was used for plays, concerts, religious and public meetings, etc. Now it sat empty unless he had business in that part of the city. When they entered what was used as the dining area, Hanani seated them and offered them refreshments. When served, Noble asked if he minded more questions.

"Not at all."

"How long have you been prophet of the city?"

"Time's hard to measure here. Each day's about the same as the last. All special days stopped when the lord of the city and his tormentors gained power years ago. I was known as the prophet then." Rue was even more amazed that she had never heard mention of him.

"Tell me about this evil lord?" continued Noble.

"He has been called by many names and titles: Satan, Lucifer, Beelzebub, the Devil, and Belial, just to name a few. Here, he has taken the name Kuriopolis, which means lord of the city. He's one you don't want to meet, but probably will. You won't have to look for him, either. He will find you. If you have encountered the tormentors, he knows that you're here, what you're here for, and who you're with," glancing at Rue. "Nothing happens in the city that he doesn't know about or is involved in. He owns or controls almost everything."

"What about the safe houses? Why doesn't he close them?" Rue asked.

"That, my child, is a mystery. My thinking is that the Higher Powers protect them. As long as there are those who desire truth and righteousness and refuse to sell out to Kuriopolis, the Higher Powers will provide for them and not forsake them." The prophet, of course, knew this to be true.

"What do you do as prophet of the city?" Rue continued.

"Back when the city thrived in the arts, my purpose was to get the religious community to appreciate the secular arts and the secular community to appreciate the beauty of religious worship. My purpose has not changed, but the longer Kuriopolis rules the city, the more difficult my job becomes. I long for a time to see the arts and religion thrive in the city again." He really did not answer Rue's question. He turned to Noble and diverted attention to their quest. "Did I hear you mention that you were looking for a man?" he asked with an intense look.

"Yes, but answer —" Hanani cut Noble off.

"Was this man brought in by force a few days ago?" he asked with a look of urgency. This was the first glimpse of hope Noble had received about his father. The prophet's diversion had worked. Rue was not going to get an answer to her question. Hanani was going to tell them what he wanted them to hear and avoid any more questions.

"Yes, I think he was. Have you seen him?" Nobel asked hopefully.

"No, but I know where they have taken him. Those that are brought in by force are taken to the high place for..." He gave Noble a hopeless look. Of course, this was bait.

"For what?" He was ready to choke the prophet if necessary. Rue had a death grip on his arm, but hardly weighed enough to hold him.

"You may not have much time. Some of the tormentors practice spilling blood to accommodate their gods. Usually, they cut themselves as sacrifice, but sometimes they use what they call innocent blood. This may be the man that you're looking for."

"Can you take us to the high places?" Noble asked.

"If they see us together, they will know where we're going and be ready. If you take them by surprise, you will have a better chance of freeing your friend."

Rue wasn't buying all of this. However, she had heard mention of high places. She spread the maps on the table looking for possible locations.

"You won't find them on the maps," the prophet said, getting up and moving toward her. "I can mark two possible locations."

"Possible locations?" she asked.

Hanani looked at the maps and said, "They move them from time to time. Believe it or not, the tormentors raid each other just for the fun of it. Who can understand the warped mind?"

He marked the maps and told them that they would recognize the paths to the high places by the small statues placed at every turn. "This is what they steal from each other to set up their worship areas," he explained. He also told them that they were usually in wooded areas. However, occasionally they would use the tops of buildings for certain rituals.

"Do you know the locations of the safe houses in these sections?" Rue asked.

"Yes, I believe so," he answered with a concern look. He realized that he had not distracted her as much as he had distracted him.

"Please mark them, and check the ones that are already marked for correctness. It will speed our travel," Rue said in a business-like manner. As Hanani marked the maps, she noticed that Noble was leaning forward in his chair looking at the inside of his shield. *She wondered how much of this* he believed. What evidence did she have against the prophet? Would the avoided questions be enough to convince him not to trust Hanani?

"May I borrow your Bible?" Noble asked the prophet.

"Yes, I believe I have one right here." He walked toward a cobweb infested desk, picked up a large, black book, wiped it off with his sleeve, and delivered it to Noble. Noble turned to Ephesians chapter six and began reading aloud at verse ten.

Be strong in the Lord and in the strength of his might. Put on the full armor of God, that you may be able to stand firm against the schemes of the devil. For our struggle is not against flesh and blood, but against the rulers, against the powers, against the world forces of this darkness, against the spiritual forces of wickedness in the heavenly places. Therefore, take up the full armor of God that you may be able to resist in the evil day, and having done everything, to stand firm.

Ephesians 6:10-13

While he was reading, Rue sat down beside him when he read verse 13, they heard a door shut behind them. They turned to look, and the prophet was gone. He looked at her and said, "I guess he couldn't stand the pressure."

Her face lit up and the fire danced in her eyes like before. She had her answer. He was not buying the prophet's story, either. She leaned on his shoulder and gave him a hug. "How did you know that he was lying?"

"I didn't. It came to me where that Scripture was on the inside of my shield, and I wanted to see what else it said."

He watched her eyes dance while being consumed by the splendor and purity of her face.

"What do we do now?" she asked.

"I don't know. How much of this information do we trust?" Noble answered a question with a question.

"Well," Rue began, "I told you earlier that I had never heard of a prophet of the city. But, I do remember some of the older ones at the safe house talking about high places. They said that at one time, the high places were places of worship for the Higher Powers alone. Natural stones and altars unshaped by human hands marked the sacred places where the creator was honored. The most sacred objects were upright uncut stone pillars. However, man began to worship the creature rather than the creator, and worship became customized to the worshiper and not limited to the Higher Powers. The craftsman could now style his gods to his own needs."

"Do you think he was telling the truth about the spilling of blood? And, if they move the high places around, how are we going to know ...." Noble's emotion began to surface as he thought about his father in the hands of the tormentors.

"I have never heard the older ones talk about the spilling of innocent blood. But moving the high places: yes."

"Not only do they move them, but the location and size become more convenient as well," said a female voice.

Noble jumped to his feet and shielded Rue from the direction the voice came. The woman called Esau had entered the room from opposite the kitchen.

She looked like she had been in a war. Her armor was marked all over, including her face and hair. She moved slowly toward them, but not too close.

"I came to warn you," she said in a calm voice, not distressed like before. "The prophet's setting a trap for you. He's probably in contact with Kuriopolis right now. Go."

"Are you all right?" Nobel moved toward her.

"I will be as soon as I find Lillith." She signaled for him to stop, raising her hand and backed away from Noble. He stopped and moved over by Rue. "I'm going to get my belt and helmet back at any cost. If I succeed, then I will help you. But now, you need to go."

"First, look at these maps and see if they're right." Noble backed away. Rue and the woman proceeded to the table. The woman scanned the maps rather quickly.

"I believe they are," said the woman.

"Was he telling the truth about the blood sacrifice?" inquired Noble.

"Yes. But I don't think he knows who has your friend. If he knew, I'd know and I don't," assured the woman.

Rue pointed to a safe house on the map. "We'll wait one day for you here, and then we're going to look for the high places." The woman agreed and turned to go.

Noble's compassion for her returned. *Had it not been for Rue, that could be me,* echoed his mind. "Would you prefer that we come with you rather than wait at the safe house?"

The woman turned and smiled for the first time since meeting them. "You have done more for me already than you know. I need to do this myself. Even if I fail, it will be better than being a play-toy for the tormentors." Her voice tightened a little, "Be on your guard. Kuriopolis is very powerful."

"We'll be praying for you," Rue said as the woman departed.

The courage that the woman saw in them reminded her of what she once had. Death would be preferable over her current miserable existence. However, refusing their help may have been a mistake. No one can make it in life entirely on their own. We all need help from time to time.

THE WAIT

CHAPTER 8

Checking the maps of the current section, they determined that they had enough light to get to the Northern safe house. Moving again, they agreed to take the woman's advice and keep their minds on their journey. Every block or two, Rue would check behind them to see if anything had changed. They paid more attention to the street intersections and the details of the buildings they passed. She even checked the tops of buildings when she turned to look behind.

They still could not see in the windows and wondered if that was how Kuriopolis kept track of everything in the city. *Were there eyes behind the bars and the glass? How did news travel so fast?* There were no signs of any phones at

Lillith's or the prophet's residence, or communication systems on the buildings.

They made it to the safe house without incident, but not before dark. However, they discovered another benefit of the shadow. As the city grew darker, the shadow illuminated their path several blocks ahead on either side and behind.

"Wow!" He turned in a circle as they moved forward.

"You say that a lot, don't you?" But she was just as taken by the attribute as Noble. This was about the distance that the robed beings were keeping as they scurried about. No doubt, they had seen shadow walkers before. Once they entered the safe house, the shadow assumed the position around the building as before. They were welcomed and fed. The evening fellowship was relaxing, but filled with new questions about the high places, the prophet, the woman called Esau, and the lord of the city.

Again, Noble found himself the center of attention, especially with the younger ones. Similar questions about his clothes and sword were posed, and he and Rue entertained them with stories and laughter. Once the younger ones were off to bed, Noble and Rue asked Eben, the overseer of the Northern safe house, if he or any of the older ones would please share anything they knew about Hanani or high places.

"Hanani calls himself the prophet of the city. I have heard that some of the other sections of the city have citizens who have taken the same title, and some have even used the same name. They work for Kuriopolis and spy on the safe houses."

"Tell us about the high places," Rue asked. "We know that they were once used to worship the Higher Powers, and they have been corrupted. But, the woman called Esau said that their location and size become more convenient. Can anyone tell us more?"

Kala, one of the older ones spoke. "The tormentors take their direction from Kuriopolis. He has changed all the rules and claims all worship, regardless of the name of the deity. No longer restricted to the summit of the hill, worship can take place on the slopes. The objects of the tormentors might be numerous and scattered over a significant area or represented by a single upright stone. The larger stones were regarded as the abode of the deity."

"Hanani said that the paths to the wooded high places would be marked by small statues," continued Rue. "But, he said that sometimes that they use buildings. How will we recognize these buildings?"

"These small statues can be carved wood or stone, and can look like man or beast," Kala continued. "There will be statues beside the entryways of the building. At one time, the trees of the high place were sacred, and their number significant. However, once Kuriopolis and the tormentors had corrupted the city, exceptions were made. Living trees could be replaced by artificial trees or carved poles. Now on the tops of buildings or behind closed doors, the worship at many high places is extremely immoral.

Many of the past shadow walkers tried to compromise with these practices, but with little success. When used for the worship of other gods, the high places destroy lives rather than strengthening the worshiper. When the worship of the Higher Powers in the high place was intermixed with heathenish practices, their continuance was the eventual cause of the darkness that has come to pass and the tormentors that have populated the city."

Noble, Rue, and the older ones shared information well past midnight. Eben gave instruction and left messages for those in charge of breakfast to plan a late breakfast. Most in the safe house would sleep late anyway, being up most of the night. Noble and Rue didn't mind. They were going to wait for the woman called Esau anyway.

Not long after he dosed off, howling and shrieking woke Noble. Flashes of light accompanied by ghastly screams assaulted his second floor sleeping quarters. He jumped out of bed, quickly dressed, hurried down the hall to Rue's room, and knocked on the door.

"Rue, are you ok?" Noble asked.

"Yes. Come on in."

Entering the dark room, the silhouette of his companion facing the window illumined as flashes strobe light into the room. Noble carefully felt his way through the darkness and joined her at the window. Arms folded, she stepped to the side and leaned against the window frame, making room for Noble to watch the bazaar ranting and raving on the ground below.

"What are they doing, Rue?"

She didn't answer. Silently, they both watched bustling dark figures aimlessly throwing flaming darts into the shadow and at each other. Chanting some kind of unintelligible song, a tormentor would throw a barrage of darts toward the house. Becoming outraged that the flames would extinguish and the darts drop to the ground before making contact, the crazed figure would charge the shadow, screaming, hands blazing with another torrent of darts, only to become more frustrated by the shadow's defenses. More often than not, the charging tormentor infringed the shadow's perimeter and suffered the consequences. Dancing away and shaking their hands frantically, the chanting would begin again and eventually the tormentor would repeat the attack.

Noble became so engrossed in the insanity that he didn't notice Rue's emotion. Tears slowly made their way to her cheeks. When she reached to wipe her eyes, her movement caught his attention.

"Rue?"

She wiped her eyes, turned away from the window, and leaned against the wall.

In a solemn tone, she began; "Since I can't hide it any more, I guess I should tell you one of the reasons why I'm helping you find your father. Some citizens very close to me were deceived by Kuriopolis and became tormentors," her voice full of emotion, Rue paused before continuing. "I have seen the elderly left homeless, with no one to care for them. I have also witnessed very young children wondering the streets crying for their mommy and daddy. Anything I can do stop this madness in my city has my full attention."

When Rue finished speaking, Noble offered a comforting arm. She accepted. Rue leaned her shoulder into his chest and rested her head on his shoulder. From the safety of the second floor window, Noble watched what her world had become. Quietly consoling his friend, sounds of the madness below mocked the broken heart of his companion. As her tears moistened his shoulder, Noble truly found what his armor and shadow would not protect him from.

Tommy's eyes were moist and his chin was quivering. Grandpa had touched a tinder spot in both their lives.

"Go ahead Grandpa, I'm okay. I was just thinking about Grandma."

"I know. Not a day goes by that I don't think about her. We both miss her."

The old gentleman looked around at the peaceful scene. The quiet waters of the lake joining the sloping banks: the cattails swaying as birds land and take flight; pines and oaks reaching for the blue sky as birds circle high above their outstretched limbs.

"Tommy, I see a perfect spot for this old man to stretch his legs and eat lunch. Would you join me?"

"Sure."

The two fishermen reel in and row ashore. With the boat secure, lunches were carried to a shady retreat. Before sitting to eat, Grandpa twisted and stretched some of the kinks from his aged body. Sitting with legs crossed and leaning against a tree, Tommy bit into his peanut butter sandwich.

"Grandpa, you can tell some more of the story if you want to."

Grandpa laughed. "Okay. Let me get situated and a couple of bites of my sandwich."

Grandpa stretched out in the warm grass and continued the story.

Rue finally said, "We need to get some sleep, if we can."

"Do you want me to sleep in the chair?"

"No. I'm fine. Go get some sleep." Rue looked out the window again. "I know it will be hard to sleep tonight. Pray that this has nothing to do with the woman confronting Lillith."

Noble put his arm around Rue's shoulders, gave a gentle squeeze, then headed back to his sleeping quarters.

The tormentors howled and clamored until morning. Most in the safe house were up all night.

Rue figured that he could not sleep. So at about dawn, she knocked on his door.

"Come on in. I'm awake."

"I didn't think you would be sleeping."

"No, I can't quit thinking about last night and the woman. I prayed for her safety and success while trying to fall asleep, but the thought keeps coming back that we should have insisted on escorting her to Lillith's."

"I prayed, too, and that's all we can do. This is a new day. Yesterday's over and can't be changed," she said almost casually. She was practical to the point of annoying at times.

"That's not all that kept me awake. You mentioned one of the reasons that you were helping me. Rue, does Kuriopolis have your parents? Were you one of the children crying in the street?

Rue walked to the window and stared into the distance. "No to both questions," she finally said. "And if you're going to ask for the rest of my reasons, today is not the day for your answers." She turned toward him and smiled. "But today's a day to keep seeking."

S*he did it again,* he said to himself. He shook his head and grinned as he joined her at the window. She had a way of calming him down and getting him to focus on the moment. They spent a quiet morning together until called for breakfast.

On their way to breakfast, Noble realized that he had been so caught up in the conversation the night before that he forgot to mention the woman before evening prayer began. Once everyone was seated at the table, he mentioned the woman and asked them to pray for her.

"Rue and I met a woman yesterday called Esau. I don't think that's her real name, but please pray for her this morning. She was with a man named Hanani, who called himself the prophet of the city. She was once a shadow walker, and is now trying to regain her helmet of salvation and belt of truth from a tormentor named Lillith."

All agreed and prayer began. Each person who wished could praise God with a sentence or two about his character. The next time around the table, a sentence or two was said about a sin that the individual struggled with. Next, they would thank God for a blessing that they had received. The last time around, they would pray for each other and they not only mentioned the woman, but the shadow walker and the guardian.

This prayer style was common at the safe houses. There was some diversity from house to house, but they always praised God first, then confessed, and gave thanks for what was, and then prayed for what could be. This was the order at every meal for young and old alike.

He was so elated with the prayer that he could hardly eat. Being part of something so wonderful usually pushes physical concerns out of the way, such as food or sleep, and feeds your spiritual part. He was not as tired as he thought he would be after the long night.

Following breakfast, the long wait began. The maps were eventually brought out and plans were discussed involving their next move. Counsel from the group was welcomed and taken with gladness. Noble talked more with Kala while Rue looked at the maps with Eben.

"If you go due south from here," Eben pointed," and then turn east about here, you should run straight into the eastern safe house. Or, this way's the more direct route," he pointed again. "However, the direct route takes you through a more residential area. The streets are winding and the lines on the map indicate elevation change. The other way's city and more flat. I'm not trying to tell you which way to go," Eben said apologetically. "It depends on what you want to look for."

"It's okay, Eben. Thank you. We'll take all the help we can get," Rue assured.

Noon rolled by with no sign of the woman. Noble toiled with the idea of returning to Lillith's. Foolishly, he expressed this thought aloud, only to receive objection not only from his companion but also from Eben.

"Rue, we should have insisted that we go with her. She should have been here by now," Noble said as he paced.

"I agree that we should have gone with her. She may have made a foolish and prideful choice. But your pacing and worrying won't help her. It won't change a thing," Rue advised.

"So, what am I supposed to do. Sit calmly and wait?"

"Yes." Rue stepped directly in Noble's path and looked him square in the eye, demanding his full attention. "Yes," she repeated, "you're to sit calmly and wait."

Noble knew that she was right, but his manliness had been challenged. The stare down lasted only a few seconds when with clenched teeth he said, "I'm going to Lillith's."

Turning hastily, Noble stepped face to face with Eben, Kala standing right beside him.

"Before you leave, "Eben began, "please listen to what I have to say." Noble stepped back out of the elderly gentleman's face, showing some respect. "The woman named Esau made her choice for whatever reason, good or bad. That's no reason for you to make a bad choice. If you would have left early this morning and ran most of the way, you would not likely have arrived before she confronted Lillith. Are you going to leave without Rue? With her injuries as near healed as they are, she's still in no shape to run that far. And with what you have seen of Peiratopos so far, do you think it's wise to go alone?

Noble closed his eyes and took a deep breath. He knew that Eben was right. He knew Rue was right. He also knew that he owed his companion an apology.

"Rue," he said, his voice tightening a little, "I had no right to speak to you like that. Please forgive me."

"You're forgiven, mighty warrior." Noble didn't have to look. He knew that she was grinning.

96

Eben grasp Noble's shoulder and said, "You're a good man, Noble. But, the evil in this city has destroyed many good men and women. Be careful. And listen to your companion."

"Thank you, Eben. I will," Noble replied.

Kala motioned for Noble to follow. "Come on Noble, before you get into any more trouble. I have a stash of banana bread in the kitchen. I'll share it with you."

After some warm banana bread and some hot tea, Rue found Noble sound asleep in his favorite place: an overstuffed chair. She smiled and thought, *I'll let him sleep until mealtime. Kala did a good job keeping him out of trouble.*

When the call for the evening meal came, Rue sat on the arm of the chair and gently woke the sleeping warrior.

"Hey. You're going to miss dinner."

"Mmmmm. How long have I been out?" Noble asked, finally stirring awake, yawning and stretching.

"An hour or so."

"Wow. I needed that after last night."

"Yes you did. You were a grumpy old bear. It's a good thing you chose to go out on your own. I was ready to knock you out."

Noble wrapped his arm around Rue's waist and stood up, lifting her off the arm of the chair, and headed for the dining room. "You might want to grow a little before you try that," he smiled.

"Put me down, you idiot!" Rue said forcefully, but enjoying every minute of the horseplay.

After the evening meal, Eben invited Noble, Rue, and Kala to join him in his quarters. Following him to the back of the house and down a flight stairs, Eben's quarters consisted of three rooms: a small but full kitchen, a bedroom with a half bath, and a room he called the snoozing room. The snoozing room had a recliner on each side of a freestanding fireplace and a couch that faced the fireplace and recliners.

"We can crowd around the table in the kitchen, or we can sit in here. This is the snoozing room. When it's cold out, I build a fire in the stove and snooze while trying to read," Eben explained.

"The snoozing room's fine," Rue replied. "We'll take the couch and I'll try to keep Noble awake."

"Kala, entertain our guests while I make some tea."

"No, no. You entertain the guests and I'll make the tea. I've had your tea before." Eben and guests laughed as Kala made her way to the kitchen.

Eben seated himself and softly said, "I never have to make tea anymore."

The three engaged in casual conversation until Kala joined them. "The tea will soon be brewing. Eben, what's the secret meeting about?"

"Nothing in particular. When was the last time we had guests? I thought that you and I, being the oldest ones in this safe house, should pull rank and selfishly enjoy some entertaining."

"Agreed," Kala said. "I had to threaten the young ones so that Noble could take a snooze this afternoon."

"I wondered how that happened," Rue said.

"Thank you, Kala. I was wound pretty tight today. The nap sure helped."

"The Rum in the banana bread works every time," Kala laughed. "Just kidding."

Noble laughed, and then said, "Again, I apologize to all of you for my actions today. I just feel like that I really messed up by letting her face Lillith alone."

"Understandable, Noble," Eben replied. "I'd doubt your credibility as a shadow walker if you didn't feel that way."

"Don't count her out yet," Kala added. "She may be on her way as we speak. If she had to hunt for Lillith, that would delay her arrival."

As they sat discussing the woman called Esau, the teapot called for attention. Eben helped Kala serve the tea. While they were in the kitchen, Rue spoke with Noble privately.

"We'll have time to make plans once she gets here," she assured him. "*What if*, doesn't help us. I know that you're concerned for her and your father, but all we can do is pray and wait," she said to him. "Worry won't help her, it will only hurt you. Let's relax and enjoy this evening so our minds will be sharp tomorrow."

He agreed.

Eben carried a serving tray from the kitchen. "Tea is served, my young friends. I watched Kala brew it, Noble. There's no Rum in it."

Eben and guests enjoyed a pleasant evening of conversation and laughter. Thoughts of evil lords, tormentors, and eminent danger slowly drifted from Noble's mind. However, sipping warm tea in a relaxed atmosphere, Noble inevitably found it impossible to keep his eyes open. Rue nudged him with her elbow.

"Noble, are you going to stay with us?"

"Mmm. No. I think I need to go to bed. Stay and visit. I can find my way." Standing, Noble thanked Eben and Kala for the evening and made his way to his room.

As he prepared for bed, his mind was eased by thinking how blessed he was to have Rue as his comrade and friend. The groups at both safe houses displayed great respect for her and her ideas. *Why shouldn't they,* he thought, *she's usually right.* He vowed that he would pay more attention to her and her advice. *At times, she shines almost as bright as the shadow does at night.* Quiet thoughts and the enjoyable evening helped him quickly fall asleep.

Awakened from a deep sleep by flashes of light and howling, Noble sat straight up and for a moment was totally disoriented.

"Not again tonight," he said aloud. "I have only been asleep a couple of hours!" He tried his best to ignore them, but sleep was next to impossible. He thought about Rue and wondered if she was sleeping. *I better go check on her.* He sat on the side of his bed with his elbows on his knees, resting his head in his hands. His body and mind ached for rest. He laid back on the bed and covered his ears with pillows and covers. It seemed like only a moment later that light was invading his eyelids. Morning had arrived.

Rue was sitting by her window when he called on her for breakfast.

"Look," she said. He walked to the window and saw the burned spots around the building. "They were really disturbed last night. I saw them pushing and throwing one another into the shadow. The group said that they hadn't been this hostile for a long time. Something major happened or is about to happen soon."

"Maybe the woman made them mad by getting her armor back." He expected to get a lecture about speculation again, but she was somber. He had never seen her like this.

"That would upset them, I suppose. I pray it's true," she said and turned away from the window.

"Did you get any sleep last night?" Noble asked.

"Yes, some: enough I suppose."

"Good. I started to come check on you but fell back asleep."

"That's okay. You needed rest. The last two days have been pretty full."

"The strangest days of my life; actually, I don't feel too bad, considering."

Breakfast call came, and they joined the group. No sign of the woman, so prayers went up again. Breakfast was quiet that morning.

Preparations were made to depart, but not with much enthusiasm.

"Do you have everything you need?" Kala asked.

"Checked, double checked, and triple checked," Rue said. "We have waited the agreed time, but it's Noble's decision to leave or stay."

"He has a big heart, Rue. Guard him well." Kala hugged Rue and left the kitchen. She found Eben and Noble discussing his departure. She slipped her arm around his waist and gave him a squeeze. "There's banana bread in Rue's pack. Share it."

"Yes, ma'am," Noble said with a grin.

"You listen to Rue. The evil in Peiratopos is very cunning. You pay attention to her and listen for that inner voice."

"I promise. Thank you, Kala."

Rue came from the kitchen and stood beside Eben. She looked at Noble and asked, "What have you decided?"

"I want to wait, but I know we can't. We need to keep searching. Eben suggests that we take the city route. We could possibly run into...it would have been nice to know her name. How long would that have taken?"

"I agree. We should have asked for her name. It would have been nice to pray for her using her real name." Rue then turned her attention to Eben and Kala. "Thank you for your hospitality and your help."

With more hugs, the travelers departed.

Without delay, Rue reminded him of the hour. "Forget the woman. Forget home. Concentrate on now. Be ready when it comes, whatever it will be."

"Right," he agreed, keeping his vow. And trouble was just around the corner.

TALL, DARK AND LOATHSOME

CHAPTER 9

They walked all morning unobstructed. Just before noon, they noticed that activity all around them had increased. They also noticed that not all the creatures were dressed alike. Besides the usual robed ones, there were some dressed like the visitors in the park. They wore the faded, multicolored suits, and some like Lillith, as well as, the prophet.

"Here we go," Noble said.

"Don't say 'stay close,' you will be wasting your breath." Were they close to a high place? Was an attack inescapable?

"Let's change course and see what happens." Noble took Rue by the hand. They made a turn at the next intersection toward the heaviest activity and received no resistance from the shadow. They quickened their pace, as their company became more agitated.

"Are they mocking us?" she asked.

"Could be," he answered. "I almost want them to do something and get it over with."

Rue was looking over her shoulder about that time and said, "Be careful what you ask for. Here they come." Tormentors of all kinds were coming from behind. They also began closing from the front and right side.

"Well, let's give them what they want," he said as he began to make a left turn. The shadow did not cooperate this time. It was time to stand.

The tormentors showed no mercy, and neither did the shadow. The sound of flaming darts and screaming became deafening. As quickly as it began, however, the battle stopped. When the smoke and stench of burnt flesh cleared the air, a smooth, deep voice broke the silence.

"Magnificent. Very impressive," said a male voice. On their left, a towering man stood alone. In a long coat covering a dark suit with gold pinstripes, black shining shoes, and hair to match, stood Kuriopolis. "You have made it farther than most," he said with a grin, "A splendid, awe-inspiring performance, *Mr.* Noble and Joanna Rue." His voice dropped even deeper. "Reminds me of a young man who once had great dreams. Yes, a very extraordinary young man predestined for greatness. That extraordinary young man is you, Noble. But, you think that because life treated you so badly that your dreams are not true." Kuriopolis turned and addressed the crowd of tormentors and prophets. "His father left his mother and Noble felt so alone."

Some of the tormentors said, "Awwwww," while others laughed.

"And now," Kuriopolis pointed, "you nasty tormentors have captured his new father and brought Noble's wrath upon me!" Fire flew from Kuriopolis' finger and hit a group of tormentors. They screamed and danced, turned and ran away in pain and terror.

"Now look at him!" Kuriopolis pointed at Noble, slowly moving closer while scolding the rest of the tormentors and prophets. "Not even *I* can change destiny!" Kuriopolis turned toward Noble and Rue, continued moving slowly, getting even closer to the shadow. "Your dreams are true, Noble. You *are* great and powerful." Kuriopolis turned to the crowd and asked, "But it's not because of his clothes, is it?"

"Nooo!" they all shout in unison.

"You're right," turning back to Noble. "It's not because of his clothes as I'm about to prove." Kuriopolis stood facing Noble with his arms open, palms turned upward, in a non-threatening posture. The tips of his black gleaming shoes seemed to touch the edge of the shadow. With a sad expression and a sheepish grin, he said, "I'll trade your father for your clothes. You win."

"Deal," Noble said.

Rue screamed horrified, "Noble! No!" But, it was too late. The deal was made.

Noble began to remove his helmet of salvation. Kuriopolis plunged his right arm up to the elbow past the perimeter of the shadow reaching toward Noble and his arm ignited.

105

"Arrrrrrr!" With teeth clenched and face contorted, Kuriopolis growled, pain racing up his arm. Fire shot from his fingertips and enveloped Noble's head. The impact knocked Noble backwards. Landing on his back with a thud, his helmet landed behind him and began to roll away.

"Nooo!" Rue shrieked. She dove for the helmet as tormentors began to shout and cheer. She scrambled back to Noble's motionless body and pushed the helmet on his singed head. Tears rolled down her face. Darts filled the air along with hideous laughter. She pulled the shield over them and began to pray.

"Quite impressive," laughed Kuriopolis as he turned away, coat sleeve smoldering. "We'll meet again, if you live."

It seemed like hours that she lay listening to screaming and laughter. Darts, smoke, and stench again filled the air. Eventually, the mood of the tormentors grew worse. They became more aggressive and sounded closer. There was more screaming than laughter. *Was it almost over? Was his shadow growing dim as his life slipped away? Would his armor soon be a prize of Kuriopolis and her a toy for the tormentors? I'd rather be dead,* she thought, ripping the sword from its sheath. *If they get past the shadow, I'll take a few of them with me.*

The screaming grew very intense, and then stopped. She did not move, waiting to be grabbed. Jumping to her feet with sword ready to strike, she saw nothing but a shadow walker adorned with long blond hair. They were in the woman called Esau's shadow.

Dropping the sword, Rue fell to her knees thanking the creator and began to attend to Noble. Hands trembling, she gently searched her fallen warrior for signs of life. Finding a pulse, Rue turned to the woman and gave an assuring nod. With tears flowing and lips trembling, Rue leaned down and kissed Noble on the cheek. The woman kneeled, put her arm around Rue, and said, "Let's get him back to the safe house."

"Speaking of getting back, we're pretty close to our limit for today. Let's go in and fix some of these beauties for supper."

The sun had moved to the western sky. The pinks and purples on the horizon were crystal clear, absent the smog of the city. The small boat carrying two fishermen made its way to where it had begun that morning. As they docked the boat, Butch met them and inspected the catch.

"What do you think, ol' boy? Is there enough for all of us, or is Tommy going to be hungry tonight? He had me telling a story out there. I couldn't concentrate on my fishin'." Butch seemed to laugh right along with them as he wagged his tail, and Tommy patted his gray head.

Grandpa cleaned the fish and fried them for supper. Tommy brought in wood for the fire and cleaned the ash from under the grate. He even helped Grandpa with the dishes without being asked. With all the evening chores finished, Tommy began getting ready for bed.

"What's this? Why are you in such a hurry for bed tonight?"

"So you can tell me more of that story."

"What story?" Grandpa teased.

"Come on Grandpa, you know what story. I gotta know what happens next."

"Okay. Let me see if Ol' Butch is ready." They both look toward the corner of the cabin where the gray-faced dog lay. He is sound asleep. "Yep. He's ready." They both laughed.

Grandpa sat down in the old chair next to the cot and began.

A TIME TO HEAL

CHAPTER 10

It was late afternoon by the time they arrived at the safe house. Quick attention was given to Noble, almost as if they were expected. Eben and Kala assisted the safe house medical personnel from the moment they received word of his return. Abby and Rue waited for word on his condition in Kala's quarters, just down the hall from where Noble was being treated. He had not regained consciousness during the awkward trek back.

During the trip, the woman introduced herself as Abby. Rue was so shaken that she had to ask Abby her name repeatedly as they talked. "If only I had just been quicker to speak. I knew better than to listen to what he was saying," she said, referring to Kuriopolis' deceptive praise of Noble.

"It was as if no matter what he said, we would have had to believe it. By the time my mind cleared, it was too late." Tears welled as Rue rehearsed the scene.

Kala entered her quarters with news about Noble. "Well, he came around for a few minutes, and now he's sleeping. That's the good news. The bad news is, he's not going to have a good hair day for a while," Kala smiled. "He's going to be fine."

Rue couldn't speak. Tears rolled down her face. Abby wrapped her arms around Rue and held her as she sobbed. Abby did not leave Rue's side that evening. When word passed through the safe house that he was sleeping rather than unconscious, all offered prayerful thanksgiving.

Enjoying a light snack, Abby and Rue tried to relax by engaging in casual conversation. However, the subject eventually returned to their situation. Rue finally asked Abby about her reason for coming to the city.

"I came to the city for the challenge. I met a person who told me about the rewards of finishing the journey. They also told me about the tricks and traps, and the battle not against flesh and blood, but darkness and evil. I had never heard of anything so intriguing. Unfortunately, I didn't make it very far before I lost a battle over power and greed. I guess part of why I came was about power: power to overcome anything I encountered in the city and then leave a heroine. But I know now that it's not about power or greatness. It's about a concern for others and walking in 'his' shadow. When I sold my belt and lost my helmet and shadow, I also lost a friend, Belor, one like you, who's now a prisoner of Kuriopolis. My greed for power cost him his freedom as well as my own." Rue was now consoling Abby as she began to cry. They continued talking about their adventures until well past midnight. When fatigue finally caught up with them, they checked in on Noble and then went to bed.

If the tormentors were active during the morning hours, our female travelers could not prove it. They slept way past breakfast. Rue awoke, coming from a deep sleep to fully awake in seconds. For a moment, she did not know where she was. Had she dreamed the day before? Did it really happen? Out of bed and dressed in a flash, she went to check on Noble. Rue met Abby coming out of his room.

"I was on my way to wake you," she said, smiling. "He's doing great. He will be ready to go in no time."

Rue quietly stood beside the bed looking down on the burnt face of her warrior. His hair was a singed mess. The redness in his face glistened from the aloe. He finally opened his eyes and smiled.

"You look terrible," Rue grinned, but tears had begun to form.

"Thanks. I hope I look better than I feel." When Rue didn't respond, Noble said, "I hear you saved my life."

Rue was now trembling, tears streaming down her face. "I thought I had lost you, Noble," she said, voice cracking.

"Thank you, but I'm not going anywhere," he grinned. "I still have answers to seek. Besides, I'm sure you haven't used up all your witty babble. And I wouldn't want to miss any of that."

"You ladies sit with him a while. I'm going to bring us back some breakfast," Kala said.

"Thank you, Kala," Rue replied.

Noble would talk with them and then fall asleep, as if it was taking all his energy to concentrate. Once Kala returned and they finished breakfast, they decided to let him sleep and occupy their time planning for when he would be ready to continue.

"Abby, what should our next move be? You obviously know the city better than I do. Hanani said that the tormentors moved the high places. Can you find them if they're not where Hanani marked them on our maps?" Rue asked.

"Yes," Abby assured. "We'll find the high places. But our next move doesn't involve hunting for them just yet. I doubt that Noble's father has been taken to a high place."

"Are we going to rescue your friend Belor and Noble's father first? If what Hanani said about the spilling of innocent blood is true, shouldn't that be our priority?"

"If what I have heard is true, Kuriopolis has no shortage of innocent blood. Hanani told me that half the city's population is in captivity. I just don't know where. But, when Noble's up to traveling, I will learn the location of the high places and the location of the captives.

I know a person not far from here who will know their location. He doesn't know it yet, but he's going to be a great help," Abby said with a grin.

Rue sat quietly for a moment. "What if Noble can't continue. Can the two of us free the captives?"

"I don't know," Abby said with a concerned look. "Three would have a better chance, but certainly no guarantee. The one thing I know that Hanani said that was true; we need to surprise them. If Kuriopolis knows that we're coming, I don't think we'll have a chance."

They both sat quietly in thought for a few minutes.

"Rue, you need to know something before you agree to go any farther on this journey," Abby said seriously. "I won't be Kuriopolis' prisoner or a play toy for the tormentors again. Do you understand what I'm saying?"

"I understand. I have watched this madness destroy lives and make the elderly and children homeless. I have felt the burn of the tormentors' darts. Yesterday, I thought that I had lost Noble, and would be a captive of Kuriopolis myself. He has my full attention, if you understand what *I'm* saying."

Abby grinned. "Yes, I do, Rue."

The next morning, Noble was up before anyone else looking for food. He was not moving very fast, but he was moving. When Rue did not find him in bed, she woke the rest of the house with a shout of joy. For once in her life, she ended up in the kitchen not looking for food. When she arrived and saw him on his feet, she did not know whether to laugh or cry. She wanted to jump in his arms, but in his weakened condition, she just stood there trembling. He turned slowly toward her, smiled, and said, "Are you hungry?"

Tears and laughter came at the same time. She could not stand still any longer. They almost landed on the floor when she wrapped him up in a bear hug and began to kiss his whole face.

"Pull her off me," he said jokingly as others entered the kitchen.

"It's about time," came an unexpected voice.

"Noble, the woman we waited for arrived just in time. This is Abby," Rue said when she turned him loose. "We owe her our lives."

Abby was more calm and serious than Rue, but tears were still in order. "Thank you," was all Noble could choke out as they embraced.

It was time to celebrate. The praise at breakfast went on until the food was almost cold, but no one complained. Following breakfast, he was brought up to date on Abby.

"After I left you at the prophets' house, I headed straight for Lillith's. I didn't expect to find her there, but I checked, anyway. However, I did find my helmet in her trophy case. She had my belt with her, trying in some way to misuse it to gain a position of power. My next stop was the basement of the city building. The tormentors use it to store their plunder. I found her trying to regain her strength from the rejection you gave her. She had my belt with her. Thanks to your stand, she wasn't hard to overpower. Lillith's now back where she belongs, running for cover with all the other tormentors. Once I had my belt and helmet in place, by his grace I was placed in his shadow again. Then finding you was easy. All I did was follow the Shadow." Abby's voice was showing signs of the moment, being an emotional time for them all. Rue then picked up the story.

"When Kuriopolis hit you with the biggest fiery dart I ever saw, your helmet landed behind us. I grabbed it, slipped it back on you, and covered us with the shield just before the darts began to fly. It sounded like the tormentors kept getting closer. I pulled your sword, and just as I was about to do something very foolish, Abby's Shadow cleared the area."

After a time of reflection, Noble broke the silence. "It was as if I had to believe everything he said," he told them as he stared straight ahead at nothing. "Like his every word caused my dreams to have meaning," he said, contemplating Kuriopolis' speech. Rue asked him to explain the dreams. He told them how he could remember details of being someone distinguished and even shared a few of his dreams with them. "I need to lie down for a while," he said. All the excitement had worn him out.

"You're not getting out of my sight." Rue slipped his arm around her shoulder and headed for his room. "You're welcome to join us, Abby."

"I think it's time to pay a visit to my friend that I was telling you about." Abby grinned. "You guys get some rest. I'll send for you when I get back." Rue assisted Noble to his room and they were both asleep before Abby looked in to say goodbye.

When Abby returned, she sent word for her two friends to join her in a private room. When they arrived, she was standing behind a man seated at a table. He was dressed in the same attire as the prophet that Noble and Rue had met earlier. "Allow me to introduce Hanani, prophet of the city," she said.

Noble replied, "Why am I not surprised that this makes perfect sense to me," being facetious, pulling chairs out for Rue and himself. Abby began to explain.

"Most of the prophets work for or are under the control of the lord of the city. He uses them to befriend travelers and direct them toward the high places. Once they search one high place and head for the other, the one they just searched is moved, and the travelers are led in circles.

Money is involved in most cases. Travelers end up paying to visit the same high places relocated and altered. But when the Hanani you met realized that you and Rue were suspicious and not going to fall into his trap, you ruined Kuriopolis' cat-and-mouse game of leading visitors in circles for profit and quickened your encounter with him. However, our new friend here, who also goes by the name Hanani in his section of the city, is going to tell us both locations of the high places as well as Kuriopolis' headquarters."

Hearing this, the man tried to break for the door. Abby grabbed him by the shoulders and slammed him back into his seat. She did not say a word but kept her hands on his shoulders, slowly moving them toward his neck. Rue whispered to Noble, "I like her." Noble locked eyes with the man. With Abby's hands moving closer and closer, the man said, "Wait! What's in it for me?"

Rue spoke immediately. "We'll let you live," she said, fixing her gaze upon him as well. The man knew who he was dealing with. This loosened his tongue into a liquid state. They got all the information they wanted and would not have any problems finding the high places and Kuriopolis' headquarters. This would give them the element of surprise, they hoped. The man was then placed in custody at the house so he could not warn Kuriopolis. Plans were then made to leave in the morning, depending on Noble's condition.

Grandpa stretched and yawned. "This is a good place to stop. We can continue the story tomorrow on the lake just like today or when we get back from fishing. I'll leave it up to you." Tommy agreed. He was pretty tired, too.

WALK ON

CHAPTER 11

The morning came for the fisherman as quickly as the one before. They had both slept soundly and were ready in record time to catch their supper. The morning air was chilly, but the day promised to be as beautiful as the day before. Since they had an early start and no bad weather was predicted, Grandpa went to a spot further down the lake where Tommy had never fished before. "This is a new place for you. Maybe I'll be able to out-catch you today," Grandpa teased Tommy.

Grandpa steered the boat to a tree that had fallen into the lake. The trunk of the tree rested on the rock ledge that formed a canopy several feet above the water. Grandpa had used this natural shelter many times. The hot sun or a hard rain can take the fun out of fishing. However, the natural shelter was not the old fisherman's target. He tied the boat so that they could fish near that submerged treetop.

Hooks baited and lines in the water, with the anticipation of that first tug; the stillness broken only by birds singing and squirrels chattering, but it wasn't long until Tommy asked Grandpa to continue the story.

"A good night's sleep can do wonders after a hard day's fishing." Grandpa acted like he didn't hear Tommy's request to continue the story. "I feel pretty good today."

Grandpa paused, waiting for a protest. "And a good night's sleep can do wonders for a shadow walker." The elderly man leaned back and crossed his legs on the seat in front of him just as Tommy's pole almost bent double.

"Get the net, Grandpa!"

The day continued as the day before with storytelling and fishing.

Noble was up and ready before his companions were even awake. As usual, he had his prayer and meditation. But this morning was different. His awareness was fresh and new. Everything around him seemed brighter and sharper somehow. His prayer was more like a conversation than ever before. While he read, meditated, and listened for the Spirit to bring God's word to his mind, scripture was clearer and more alive than ever before. It was like being in a beautiful meadow of flowers and grass with a gentle breeze and sunlight filling the day. *Better than any dream I ever had,* he thought.

When he picked up the shield, the passage inside called out for review. While he read the passage again and again, he discovered its' focus centered on "speaking in boldness". *This must be something I'm going to need soon. I had better keep it ready.*

Someone knocked on his door. "Come in," Noble said.

"Good morning, Noble," Eben smiled. "You're up early. How do you feel?"

"Eben, I feel great."

"Good. I'm glad to hear that. You recovered rather quickly."

"Oh, I still hurt. But," Noble paused, searching for the right words, "it's hard to explain. Something's different. Reading scripture this morning, and my prayer; everything seems brighter and more alive somehow."

Eben grinned. "That's what I came to talk to you about. Do you understand what's happening to you?"

"Yes and no, I think," Noble grinned. "I'm listening."

Eben laughed. "Let's sit down. This might take a while." Noble sat on the edge of the bed. Eben leaned back in the chair beside the bed and continued:

"People come to faith at all ages, from very old to quite young. Some think that when they come to faith that life from that point forward should be perfect: no faults, no problems, and no temptations. Actually, the opposite's true. Life becomes more difficult because the individual has stepped out of darkness, where Kuriopolis has control, and into the light, where the powers of darkness do not want them to be. So a battle for the mind begins. When

Kuriopolis talked about your dreams, he stroked your pride, didn't he?"

Noble dropped his head and grinned. "Yes he did."

"He knows our weaknesses. All of our weaknesses fall into one of three categories: lust of the flesh, lust of the eye, or pride of life. Kuriopolis has used the same tactics since the beginning of time."

Noble sat quietly, thinking about his encounter with Kuriopolis. "Why didn't my shadow or shield protect me?"

"They did protect you. We wouldn't be having this conversation if they didn't. You made the choice, and the choice will always be yours to make, to make a deal with darkness. You chose to compromise your gifts. You didn't listen for your inner voice or wait for Rue to speak, did you?

"No, I didn't."

"Have you learned anything from your experience?" Eben grinned.

"Yes, sir. I sure have," Noble said seriously.

"Good. One more thing and maybe the most important: some would quit at this point. They would consider themselves a failure or point the finger of blame everywhere but at themselves, even blaming the shadow. But you haven't done that, have you?"

"No sir. And I won't. I know that Kuriopolis tricked me into making a bad choice. I'm not going to quit or blame anyone else.

"Very Good. Remember, Noble, your battle has already been won. The creator considers success getting up one more time than you have been knocked down. He gives the victory." Eben got up and strolled to the door. "See you at breakfast," he said and let himself out.

Noble spent the rest of the morning reading, singing, humming, and talking to God and himself.

The call for breakfast came, and the usual prayer circle began when everyone was in place. When it became his turn to speak, he said, "I realize more than ever before that it's by God's grace that I exist and move. I have encountered the greatest evil and am still alive to walk on. Even though I did not "stand firm and resist" (Ephesians 6:13), but tried to handle the situation myself, God was merciful and will allow me another chance.

Grandpa paused and adjusted the slack in the rope that held the boat to the tree. "Tommy, from the world's point of view, he had failed. He was finished. He would never get past this and be a winner. But from God's point of view, he sees us through his Son. This truth had come alive inside him. Even if he did not make it past the next encounter with Kuriopolis, the journey to this point had been well worth its bruises. Do you understand what happened inside Noble, Tommy?"

"I think so."

"Sometimes it's the bad things that happen to us that really makes us think about life and brings the greatest amount of growth. It all depends on what you do with these bad things. Noble made the right choice." Grandpa continued the story.

"Are we ready?" Noble asked, walking out the front door and joining the group gathered around Rue and Abby. Many of the residence came out with Eben and Kala to send the travelers off bathed in prayer.

"As ready as we'll ever be, I suppose," Abby replied.

"Rue?" Noble addressed his companion with an inquisitive look.

"Kala has taken care of us," Rue said, swinging the bag onto her shoulder. "I don't think I could get another thing in my bag."

Noble smiled, embraced Kala and said, "Thank you for everything."

"Take care, Noble Shadow Walker," Kala said.

"Is that my new name?" Noble asked jokingly.

"I pray that it is," Kala replied smiling, but Noble could see the concern in her expression.

Noble looked around for Eben. As he searched the group for the overseer, some of the residence stood silently, head bowed. Others with hands lifted, looked upward, and prayed softly. Hearing the door behind him, Noble turned to see Eben flipping through the pages of an old tattered book. Without being noticed, Eben had returned inside to retrieve his Bible. He found what he was looking for, looked up, and addressed the group.

"I had no intention of making a big speech. What Noble, Rue, and Abby are attempting to do deserves more than any words that I could say. So, I choose to let Daniel speak for us. His city was in ruin for many of the same reasons as our city. Let this be our prayer. In chapter nine, verse eighteen, Daniel prays: "O my God, incline your ear and hear! Open your eyes and see our desolations and the city which is called by your name; for we are not presenting our supplications before you on account of any merits of our own, but on account of your great compassion. O Lord, hear! O Lord, forgive! O Lord, listen and take action! For your own sake, O my God, do not delay, because your city and your people are called by your name." We want our city and our people to be taken back from Kuriopolis and returned to the rightful owner. Noble, Rue, and Abby gives us hope."

Eben closed the book and joined the group in more farewells to the travelers.

MARION DAVID RUSSELL

SEEKING ANSWERS IN HIGH PLACES

CHAPTER 12

The Hanani that Abby recently introduced to Noble and Rue lived and worked the eastern section of Peiratopos. According to his information, all high places had been moved from the section the woman called Esau once worked. One was set up in his section in a wooded area near the residential section Eben previously marked on the map and would be their first stop.

Heading southeast from the Northern safe house, the travelers in single file, crossed diagonally the north/south intersections, Abby in the lead, Rue in the middle. A few blocks from the safe house, a wide street turned gently in the direction they desired to go.

"Here we go," Abby pointed. "Just like Eben said. This street takes us right into the eastern section."

"It appears to be a main street," Rue observed, as she followed Abby into the middle of the street. "Should we try to stay more hidden?"

"Good point," Abby agreed.

"Stop!" Noble said.

Abby instinctively readied her shield and said, "What?" looking all around for intruders. Not seeing any pending danger, she turned to Noble, who was looking toward the ground in the direction from which they just came.

"Look," he pointed. "Look at the Shadow." He turned in the direction of Abby and pointed toward the building on the other side of the street. "Look how big it is," as he turned and pointed all around them. From the center of the wide street, the Shadow now covered the distance from building to building and about the same distance all around them.

"Well," Rue commented, "if we had enough shadow walkers we could cover the whole city."

"That would be nice," Abby chuckled. "But, that's not the case. It appears that we have more protection now that two shadow walkers are working together. But, I like your idea of better cover, Rue. Let's stay close to the buildings."

Just past noon, they reached the first high place, right where the prophet said it would be. Rue made some comment about the prophet's life that neither Noble nor Abby could remember later. A path at the edge of the city, like the one Noble had entered on, twisted up a hill into the woods.

"I think we have surprised them," said Abby, "since we don't have any greeters. Remember what we discussed. As we go up the path ---."

"Yes," Noble said, drawing his sword, "I'll take the left side." The change in him left Rue speechless. He was more focused, confident, determined, and a few other characteristics that she could not think of at the moment.

"Ready to crash a party, Rue?" asked Abby.

"Ready."

Noble touched the stone figure with his sword. "You will have no other gods before me," he said boldly. The stone figure crumbled, and a faint scream was heard up ahead. Around the next turn was another statue on Abby's side.

"You will have no other gods before me," she said. The statue crumbled, and another scream was heard from ahead. They wound back and forth up the path, destroying statue after statue. When they reached the high place, they saw tormentors in total confusion. They were fighting each other, cutting themselves, and screaming for their gods to protect them.

"Look at that," Abby said. "They don't even know that we're here. They have no idea what's happening to them. We have caught them by surprise. Now we have to keep them from warning the others. Rue, you know what you have to do."

Taking Noble and Abby by their arms that held their swords, Rue raised them above her head and then touched the swords together. They all three shouted, "You will have no other gods before me." Flashes of colored light eliminated the faint shadows created by the noonday sun, filtering through the trees. Human like images of light formed around the perimeter of the shadow. Glistening with every color in the rainbow, the human like images appeared to be facing outward, holding flaming swords in each hand. Noble gasped.

Rue, letting go of the shadow walker's arms, folded her arms across her chest and said, "They're on our side."

"What are they?" Abby asked, but Rue didn't respond.

Frantic tormentors shielded their eyes, screaming in pain. Finally realizing the source of their pain, enraged tormentors charged Abby, Noble, and Rue. The barrage of darts that sizzled through the air came directly at Rue, passing through and around the glistening images. Shields ready, Noble and Abby sandwiched Rue between them. The sound of the darts hitting the shadow walker's shields was deafening.

Unlike the charging tormentors beneath Rue's safe house bedroom window, who tried to avoid the shadow's perimeter, the infuriated tormentors of the high place charged full speed into the shadow's glistening images. Raising their flaming swords ready to strike, the human like images intercepted the screaming tormentors. A sword crackled through the air, making contact with the first tormentor. A flash of white light completely encompassed the tormentor and absorbed him. One by one, tormentor after tormentor encountered a flaming sword and vanished. A simple description would be to say that light consumed the darkness.

With the last dart ringing off the shield and the last flash of vanishing tormentor, the glistening images resumed their positions and slowly faded. Noble and Abby watched, speechless.

Noble finally broke the silence. "What just happened?" he asked turning toward Rue.

Standing with arms folded and eyes closed, Rue trembled, tears streaming down her cheeks. Abby pulled her close, embraced her, and said, "You did what you had to. I'm sorry."

When Rue composed herself, she gently pushed away from Abby. Wiping her face, she turned toward the path they followed to the high place.

"I know I did what I had to do, and it's not going to get any easier. Let's go." She started down the path and said, "Hanani said that the second high place had been moved close to Kuriopolis' headquarters for a special ceremony."

"Wait," Noble said. Rue stopped but didn't turn around. He looked at Rue, then at Abby who was shaking her head, as if to say, *don't ask.*

Without turning around, Rue said, "What you just saw is part of the answers you still seek. For the rest of the answers, you need to keep seeking." She then continued down the path.

Leaving the residential area, they headed southwest toward the center of Peiratopos. They moved quickly through the city on the most direct route they could take.

"Look at this, Noble," Abby said. "It's the middle of the day and the streets are empty. People should be shopping, business should be open without bars on the windows, and children should be playing in their yards without the fear of being taken. Kuriopolis has brought this city to its knees because the citizens traded the creator's truth for Kuriopolis' lies."

"I hope we can change that Abby," Noble replied. "I haven't lived very long, but even in my wildest dreams, I never thought I'd see anything like this."

What a dark, dreary, lifeless city it was as the three swiftly moved closer to the high place and Kuriopolis' headquarters.

LIGHT FILLED THE DARKNESS

CHAPTER 13

Abby pointed to a four-story building with a flat roof. "I see it and I hear them," Rue said.

"Do we have to go into the building," Noble asked.

"No," Rue confirmed. "They will come to us."

"I don't see any of them in the streets. I still think we have the element of surprise on our side," Abby observed.

They marched right up to the building unnoticed. Standing in the middle of the street, Rue raised the sword-filled hands of Abby and Noble, touched the swords together, and they shouted in unison, "The light filled the darkness!" The dark windows on every floor of the building became luminous with flashes of colored light as the sword wielding images surrounded the travelers. The front entrance burst open spilling dart slinging screaming tormentors into the street. Shields ready and Rue protected, the first darts rang off the shields. Rue buried her face on Noble's shoulder and began to weep. "I can't watch," he heard her cry.

Flaming swords began crackling. As tormentors began to vanish, more poured into the street from the front entrance and from around both corners of the building.

"They're coming from the sides!" Noble screamed.

Noble and Abby's armor was now being pelted by flaming darts coming from each side. Abby turned and pressed her body against Rue, protecting her as best she could. Swords crackled, lights flashed, darts and smoke filled the air.

Mixed with the noise of shrieking rage and darts hitting shields, the sound of breaking glass raining to the street from above was followed by a chair crashing to the pavement. A tormentor jumped from a third story window, hands blazing, crippling him when he hit the pavement. Trying to stand, the fuming tormentor continued a torrent of darts while crawling to his demise.

"This is insane!" Noble shouted.

Flaming darts began ringing off the tops of their shields. Rue yelled as hot pieces of shattered dart hit her bare arm.

"They're coming from the top of the building!" Abby yelled. "Drop to your knees and put the shield over you!"

Noble dropped to one knee pulling his trembling companion with him and covered her with his shield. Abby stepped back, straddling Rue, watching the rooftop and as well as each side.

The flow of tormentors began to slow from the main entrance. "It will be over soon," Abby shouted. "They're thinning out!" Suddenly, the barrage of darts stopped from the rooftop. Noble looked up and started to stand when he saw the tormentor bound from the top of the building, hands blazing, sailing over the circle of glimmering images.

"Abby! Above you!" Noble screamed. Abby looked up and braced herself for impact. Flaming darts again rained from above. If she moved, Rue could be crushed. "I'll deflect him if I can!" She shouted.

Seconds before contact with the insane creature, a sword-wielding image sprang between Abby and the plummeting tormentor. With the crackling of a flaming sword, the threat was gone. The glimmering image remained above them, hovering, and appeared to be facing the building, until the last tormentor vanished. Turning slowly, the hovering image drifted to his previous position on the perimeter of the shadow, and with the other images in place, faded.

As the battle came to a close, Noble helped Rue to her feet. All three travelers watched the hovering image drift in place and fade. The once vacant street that moments before hosted a deafening vigorous battle now revisits the past, gripped in silence; a shattered window and a broken chair linger the only evidence. Looking around, then at each other, Abby broke the stillness.

"We may have just lost our advantage," she said. "As close as we are to Kuriopolis' headquarters, one of them was bound to hear the battle. We better get moving."

"He did this," Rue said hatefully, referring to Kuriopolis. "That lying, deceitful, vile, slithering creep did this to my city!"

With a surprised expression, Noble looked at Rue, then at Abby. Rue was no longer the sobbing, teary-eyed girl that just moments ago huddled under his shield. Forced to do what she loathed, his once witty fiery-eyed companion now harbored anger in her voice and fury in her eyes. Determined to finish what she did not start, her mission was clear, and her jaw was set. This was the city building Rue; the Rue that was ready to punch the mayor.

Rue faced the direction of Kuriopolis' headquarters and said, "Let's go."

Leaning back in his chair and propping his feet on his desk, Kuriopolis addressed the prophet Hanani. "Well my friend, we have time to discuss our problem before the sun goes down and my dancing idiots start their worship ritual."

"Sir, I can explain," the trembling prophet said. "It wasn't my fault."

"Please do. I want to know why the woman called Esau is no longer in your service."

"When I came to tell you that Joanna Rue was helping the shadow walker, and that they were not falling into our trap, Esau by some means took her belt away from Lillith. The shadow walker had to help her somehow."

"The shadow walker, Noble, was at Eben's safe house. I sent my minions to keep an eye on him. He didn't help her, you did. You let her out of your sight."

"No. The tormentors were supposed to watch her while I came to see you. They had her when I left."

Kuriopolis laughed. He got up and sauntered around the desk and put his arm around the shoulder of the trembling man. "Hanani, prophet of the city, that was not a smart move."

Hanani closed his eyes and shook his head in agreement with Kuriopolis, and in a weak voice said, "I know."

"But, that's okay. You had a bad day and I understand. I'm not upset. You know that I'm reasonable," Kuriopolis said sarcastically. Turning around, keeping his arm on the prophet's shoulder, and leading him out to the balcony, he said, "If I was upset, and not reasonable, I'd throw you off this balcony." Bending slightly over the rail and looking down, he asked the prophet, "How high do you think we are: fifteen stories maybe? OPEN YOUR EYES AND LOOK!"

Hanani opened his eyes and nearly lost his lunch.

"Awww. Don't be upset. I'm not going to throw you off. It would kill you instantly. Besides, I don't want you to miss my worship ceremony. I want you right by my side. See," Kuriopolis pointed, "we'll be right over there on that four-story building. And who knows? You might live when I throw you off."

As Kuriopolis held the weak-kneed prophet, he looked out over the gloomy city. All was quiet. Kuriopolis sighed. "Isn't it beautiful Hanani? My kingdom. And soon it's going to be even more beautiful. What do you think? Let's go have a drink."

"Excuse us sir." Dexios and Orthos stepped onto the balcony.

"What is it?"

"The Shadow Walkers have disrupted our worship plans."

"What! How?" Kuriopolis turns abruptly, then pauses. "Well," he said, looking at Hanani, "we must not get excited. A last minute change in plans makes for a challenge, don't you think?"

"Please, just let me go," Hanani whimpered.

"Okay." Kuriopolis grabbed Hanani's coat collar and stiff-armed him into the air. Turning back to the balcony and dangling Hanani over the handrail, he shouted emphatically, "HE WILL BE RIGHT DOWN ESAU!" his voice boomed through the city.

Looking up at the horrified prophet, Kuriopolis said, "Nah. I think I'll let you watch me kill her first. Then I'll throw you off."

Turning to Dexios and Orthos, who waited in the doorway, Kuriopolis ordered, "Alert the tormentors and get them into the streets. I want the Shadow Walkers surrounded. Detain them, but they're not to be attacked until I get there. They're *not* to get into this building. Get the model and the jars into the safe and guard them with your life. Go!"

"Yes, Sir." Dexios and Orthos turned and hurried off.

Kuriopolis turned his attention back to the dangling prophet. "This building holds the future plans for my kingdom. We wouldn't want those Shadow Walkers ruining our future, would we?" Hanani continued whimpering and trembling. "Why the sad face, Hanani? Oh. That's right. It's my future, not yours. But, I think you will enjoy the little time you have left. Let's go see your friend, Esau."

"Did you hear that?" Noble asked. Abby, Noble, and Rue stopped when they heard a voice echoing off the buildings.

"Well, Kuriopolis knows that we're here." Abby said. "Our surprise is over, so watch your back, Rue. We might as well get out in the open so we can see them coming."

"I still have a surprise for Kuriopolis," Rue said in a cold hard tone.

"What did he mean, Abby?" Noble asked. "He used the name Esau."

"I don't know, but you can bet it's not good. We better get moving." Abby took the lead with Rue in the middle.

Turning the corner and heading south, Kuriopolis' headquarters came into view. His headquarters, being quite visible, was the pinnacle of the city, a penthouse built on one of the tallest buildings. With a dome roof, the cylindrical five-story tower sat atop one of the older ornate ten-story buildings with arched stone entries and stone corners accenting the brick walls.

"There it is and here they come," Abby said.

His headquarters sat on their left about three blocks south. Smaller buildings blocked the north and south sides, but coming from the west entrance and from around the southwest corner, tormentors in a variety of clothing, drab robes as well as faded, multicolored suits, both male and female, flowed from the building. Some crossed the street and disappeared behind the buildings to the right. A group of a dozen or so scurried to the center of the street about a block north of Kuriopolis' headquarters and stopped.

"Move to the center of the street," Abby directed, "and watch for an ambush."

Remaining in single file with Rue in the middle, Abby moved with vigilance toward the waiting tormentors, scanning the buildings on her left and right, as Noble watched their backs.

From the rear, watching the streets and alleyways for activity, Noble could see a steady stream of tormentors heading north, crossing the alleys between the buildings on either side. Walking backwards most of the time, he had not noticed the change in Rue.

"Abby, we're getting company behind us," Noble said, turning in her direction. "Ahh!" Noble gasped. "Abby, Rue!" he shouted.

Abby wheeled around in a crouched defensive stance, shield ready. The surprised look on her face slowly changed to a grin as she observed the change in Rue. A translucent soft blue aura covered her from head to toe. Her eyes sparkled when they moved. The translucent aura faintly darkened her light olive skin. She was talking in a low whisper, but Abby could not understand what she was saying.

"I take it that this is part of Kuriopolis' surprise?" Abby observed.

"Kuriopolis' surprise!" Noble exclaimed. "Rue, you nearly gave me heart failure. How about a little warning next time?"

"Rue grinned, but Noble didn't see it. "Just follow my lead and listen to the inner voice when we meet Kuriopolis. And don't worry about shielding me," she instructed.

Hearing voices and chanting coming from behind, Noble turned to see tormentors nearer than he anticipated.

"Rue, what's going on with the Shadow?" Noble shouted. "The tormentors are really close." Smaller in size, the shadow no longer spanned from building to building.

"Walk beside me Noble, and get ready for Kuriopolis," Rue said calmly, not addressing his question.

Moving alongside Rue, Noble continued to watch the tormentor activity as they moved closer to Kuriopolis' headquarters. Tormentors now completely surrounded them. Coming from every alley and street intersection, tormentors lined the sidewalks and the tops of buildings. They chanted, shrieked, and laughed hideously while shouting insults and profanity, mostly at Rue.

"Rrrruuuuoooo," they would call.

"Look at the pretty blue girl," one shouted, then spit.

"She's not as pretty as PJ boy," another shouted, made some obscene gestures, and then blew a kiss.

"Why aren't they attacking?" Abby asked.

"I have no idea," Noble replied. "Rue's full of surprises. Ask her."

"I don't know," Rue answered between whispers.

As they moved closer to the group of tormentors that waited in the street, the activity and noise level grew more intense from the ones dogging them. One had a metal rod, punching it past the iron bars and breaking the glass in the storefronts. Another found a length of wood and banged signs and benches: anything they could find to make loud sharp sudden noises.

"I have never seen anything like this before," Abby commented. "And I've seen some pretty bazaar things from tormentors."

"What's going on Rue: any idea?" Noble asked.

"They're trying to break my concentration," she answered. "If they succeed, shield me."

"I know that you will tell me that this is not the time, so I won't ask, "Noble said. "But I think I now have more questions than I came in this place with."

"Indeed," Rue grinned. "Keep seeking."

The noise level increased to near deafening when the shadow finally reached the group of tormentors that blocked the street.

"Should we stop or push them back?" Abby asked.

"Stop," Rue said. "It's Kuriopolis' move."

When they stopped, several of the tormentors were pushed into the shadow by the momentum of the following crowd. Having no room to move, the screaming tormentors burned and smoked until they fell lifeless.

The circle of tormentors seemed to become more energized with the demise of their comrades. Frantic movement in the tight packed crowd resulted in more contact with the shadow. Tormentors on the rooftops shouted and cheered at the activity below.

Noble felt his tension building as the noise level amplified. His eyes darted from side to side, watching the prolific insanity as he waited for Kuriopolis to show. *And then what? Can we win? Do we even have a chance?*

"Ready your swords," Noble heard Rue shout. He pulled his sword and turned to face her. She raised her arm from her side and he placed his forearm in her open hand. Abby did the same. Rue then reminded them, "Listen for the inner voice and follow my lead."

A head appeared at the rear of the crowd in front of them. Pulling and pushing tormentors out of his way, Kuriopolis struggled to the middle of the psychotic mass, stopped, and bellowed, "Shut up!" Noble thought his eardrums had burst. But when the ringing subsided, the crowd was silent. He could actually hear Rue's whisper.

"Thank you. Now, move back! Give our guests some room," Kuriopolis demanded in a sarcastic tone. Scrambling out of his way, the tormentors opened a wide path between Kuriopolis and the shadow walkers. Dragging the limp body of one of the prophets, he stepped forward, pointed and motioned with his other hand for the crowd surrounding the shadow walkers to step back as well.

"Much better," Kuriopolis said. He stopped about ten feet from the perimeter of the shadow, lifted the prophet and held him like a dangling puppet. Noble couldn't tell if he was dead or in shock.

"Hanani," Kuriopolis said, "the lovely Esau has come to see you. See her pretty blond hair. But, it would be so much prettier if that helmet of salvation didn't hide so much of it. Aren't you sorry you let Esau get her helmet back?"

"The name's Abby," Abby said.

"WHO CARES!" Kuriopolis roared.

"Just for the record," Abby responded calmly.

"What record? Who's going to keep a record of this?" Kuriopolis demanded.

"You," Abby replied. "You will have plenty of time when we send you back to the Abyss where you belong."

Kuriopolis laughed hardily. "Good one," he said. "Did you hear that Hanani. Esau thinks that I'm going to break my promise to you. Stay awake now. I promised that you could watch me kill her."

"Shut up, you snake," Rue said forcefully. "You're done talking. Do what you came to do."

"How rude," Kuriopolis responded. "I haven't spoken to Noble yet."

"He's not listening," Rue replied in the same forceful tone.

"Can't the boy speak for himself?" Kuriopolis asked. "Does he have to have his smurfette speak for him now?"

Rue raised the sword filled hands of the shadow walkers over her head, touched the swords together, and continued to whisper. The sword wielding images appeared at the perimeter of the shadow as before. But, there were no screams from the tormentors or flashes of colored light anywhere. And, the images were not multicolored. They were the same color as Rue. And their swords did not point forward as those did before, but pointed to the side, crossing the sword of the humanlike image next in line, making an unbroken curve of images and swords above the shadow's perimeter.

Noble and Abby both slowly surveyed the circle in wide-eyed amazement. Rue anticipated their surprise. "Concentrate," she said. "Listen for the inner voice. The sword of the spirit will tell you what to say." She did not, however, expect to see a surprised look from Kuriopolis. He tried to hide his surprise by turning his head and speaking to the prophet.

"Well, Hanani, it looks like if I'm going to speak to Noble, I need to do it quickly. I think I smell death in the air." He looked back at the circle, pointed at Rue, and as his hand ignited, he roared, "Kill them!"

As the insanity resumed, Noble closed his eyes, making every effort to block out the screaming and hideous laughter. Resounding off the walls of the buildings and the hard pavement of the street, the repulsive sounds seemed to penetrate his body. *Concentrate Noble, listen for the inner voice*, he heard Rue's voice say in his mind. And, then he spoke.

"Resist the Devil and he will flee from you!" Noble shouted with Rue and Abby.

The sound of an explosion reverberated between the buildings and drowned out the noise of the battle. Breaking off the attack, distracted tormentors turned in the direction of the blast. Window openings on every floor of Kuriopolis' headquarters burst with multicolored light. The domed roof split as the circular tower walls atop the ten-story building began to crack vertically, releasing the dancing light.

Kuriopolis turned toward the sound of the explosion. "Aaaarrrr!" he roared, like an injured beast. "Noooo!" He started to run toward the building, but stopped after a few feet. He turned and launched the body of Hanani toward the shadow walkers and screamed at the idle tormentors who were watching the tower begin to crumble. "Kill them! Kill them!"

The shrieking war cries of battle resumed. The airborne body of the prophet sailed headlong over the Shadow's defenses, striking Rue just below the knees.

"Ahhh!" she cried. Taking her legs out from under her, Rue struggled to hang on to the arms of the shadow walkers. Though shielded by the blue aura, the impact challenged Rue's ability to concentrate. Trying to move with her as the momentum of the prophet's body drug her backwards, the swords broke contact and the perimeters defenses begin to fade.

As darts began to penetrate the fading defense, Kuriopolis charged the shadow walkers, roaring like a wild beast. Scrambling to regain her footing, Rue felt the sting of darts break through her vanishing aura.

"Shield me!" she yelled. Abby and Noble were already in motion. Still hanging on to their arms, they pulled her to her feet; then placed one shield in front and one behind. With darts singing off the shields and pelting the armor of the shadow walkers, Rue closed her eyes, touched the swords together, and began to whisper. As her aura returned, so did the perimeter defenses.

Kuriopolis hit the shielded boundary like a charging bull. The line buckled, but held. His face contorted as he screamed in pain and anger, trying to push through the defenses.

"I'm going to kill all of you!" Kuriopolis screamed. Staggering away from the shadows perimeter, doubled over in pain, Kuriopolis looked toward his collapsing tower. The vertical cracks had continued to open. The domed roof was gone. Large pieces of wall broke away and toppled to the ground. He straightened, leaned his head back, raised his

146

clenched fist to the sky, and roared. He grabbed a tormentor and turned to throw him at the shadow walkers.

Noble heard the prompting of the spirit and shouted with Rue and Abby, "You will have no other gods before me!"

The sudden deafening insane screaming of tormentors hurt Nobles ears. Scores of multicolored sword wielding images appeared randomly inside and outside the blue line of defense. Darting frantically, the bewildered tormentors wrapped their hands and arms around their eyes and ears in a futile attempt to protect themselves from the inevitable. Flaming swords crackled as tormentor after tormentor vanished.

Kuriopolis hurled the screaming tormentor at Rue. Clearing the blue line of defense, two multicolored sword-wielding images intercepted the arm-flailing projectile. Grabbing another tormentor in a fit of rage, a thunderous crash diverted his attention. Turning, he saw that a large section of tower wall was gone. Roaring in uncontrollable rage, Kuriopolis turned and wildly slung the tormentor toward the Shadow Walkers, only to drill him into the blue line of defense, killing him instantly. He then turned screaming, "I'll kill all of you," and ran into the crumbling building.

"I think it's over," Abby said, breaking the silence following the last scream. "Rue, can you please let go of my arm? My hand's numb."

Rue opened her eyes and looked around, but continued whispering. She loosened her grip on the Shadow Walkers' arms, but continued to hold them in position over her head as she surveyed the area. The multicolored images were returning from between buildings and gathering around the perimeter of the blue images. As they were all watching the human like images return, a thunderous crash startled them. They turned to see that the tower was gone, and that bricks and debris rained into the streets from the top floors of the ten-story building. A trail of dust and smoke rose into the air above the structure.

"Is he gone?" Noble asked.

The multicolored images had returned and faded. Satisfied that the perimeter defense was no longer needed, Rue lowered her arms and in between whispers said, "He's gone."

"Yes!" Tommy shouted. This gave Grandpa a start. They were both really into the story.

"This is a good place to stop. It's time we head in and clean these fish. Butch will be getting worried." Grandpa untied the boat and headed for the dock.

Once the fish were cleaned, the frying began. The smell filled the cabin with a "can't wait" aroma that even had Butch at attention. Tommy and Grandpa both ate more than they should. Tommy and Butch were out the door to enjoy the last few rays of sun dancing with the breeze in the treetops. Grandpa dried the plates and silverware, picked up his Bible, and headed for the porch swing to do the same. A couple more chapters in Romans and a few Psalms brought newness of spirit to a tired old body. The view from the porch was of a boy and a dog among the trees, exploring. A long stick became a walking staff; a short stick whirling through trees became game for a retriever. The adventure ended with the chill of the evening air and the return of the night creature's music.

Grandpa looked up from his Bible when he heard footsteps coming up the path. Closing the book, the porch swing creaked as the elderly gentleman leaned forward and rose to his feet.

"Hey Grandpa," Tommy said, breathing heavily, greeting his grandfather. "Butch let me win again. We raced from the dock."

Grandpa smiled at the boy and old dog as he made his way across the porch. Tommy trudged up the porch steps and swung the screen door open. Butch slowly followed up the steps, tongue hanging, panting briskly.

"There's not a lot of race left in Ol' Butch, I'm afraid," Grandpa replied.

The dog made his way through the open door and found his usual spot. Tommy held the door for Grandpa, and then followed, closing the screen door and entry door behind him.

Grandpa cleaned some ash from the fireplace and built a fire while Tommy readied himself for bed. Lowering himself in his old chair, Grandpa leaned his head back, folded his arms, and closed his eyes. In what seemed like only minutes, he heard Tommy climb onto the cot. He opened his eyes to see the boy cross-legged, arms folded, and grinning at him.

Grandpa smiled, leaned forward, cleared his throat, and continued the story.

MARION DAVID RUSSELL

THE DUNGEON

CHAPTER 14

"First building south past the headquarters, west corner," Abby said, reminding them as they zigzagged through the debris. The upper half of a single, windowless door came into view on the corner of the building. Debris from the explosion blocked the entrance. Minutes seemed like hours as the three tossed brick after brick into the street behind them.

"Well, Rue, I guess your prophet friend gets to live after all. His directions were right on," Abby said, breaking the silence.

"Yes, I suppose. Although I'd like to see how big his eyes could get during a good choking. Would you do that for me, Abby?"

"Maybe you will get your chance," Noble added. The bricks were now away from the door, and his delight turned to dismay. The exterior of the door was smooth, without handle or knob, and locked from the inside.

Stepping toward the door, Noble drew his sword. Rue gently touched his shoulder and said, "Allow me, mighty warrior." She placed her hands on the door where the lock would be located on the inside. Thud! The opening sound of a dead bolt lock pierced the silence. The door moved. Speechless and with eyes bugged, Noble slowly stepped back out of Rue's way. Rue caught the edge of the door with her fingers and pulled the door open.

Moans and gags broke the silence, as the smell of human waste had reached their faces.

"How could anyone live in these conditions?" Noble gagged. Abby stepped into the doorway.

"Take a deep breath and come on. Stay together. We don't know what's down here." Abby led the way, shield ready, feeling every step. After a few moments, their eyes adjusted to the soft light that the shadow and Rue was providing.

The captives were held in total darkness. Iron bars like jail cells covered cavities cut in stone on both sides of a wide walkway, descending into the earth. As they cautiously moved closer to examine the first of the cells, their shadows softly lit the cavities. The scene was heartbreaking. Bodies sat shoulder-to-shoulder, leaning against the cell wall. Ragged clothes hung on frail frames, but they were alive. When the light touched their sunken faces, hands raised to protect their eyes.

"Let's get them out of there and get out of this stinking place," Noble said. Abby was closest to the cell bars.

"We have a problem. I don't see any way to open the cells," Abby replied. There were no doors on the cells. Noble and Rue moved alongside Abby.

"How could they survive like this?" repeated Noble.

"Time's wasting, warriors. Draw your swords. The gates of hell will not prevail," Rue exclaimed. She backed away from the cell. Noble and Abby stationed themselves on each side of the opening, drew their swords, touched them against the bars as Rue instructed, and repeated the command in unison.

"The gates of hell will not prevail!"

The bars fell into the walkway as if gently pushed from the inside. The sound of the bars hitting the dirt floor brought new life to the frail frames inside the cavities. Hands that protected light deprived eyes now reached toward their rescuers.

"Praise the creator," one cried in a weak trembling voice, struggling to stand.

Stepping over the bars into the cell, Noble said, " Help me get them on their feet, Abby."

Abby helped Noble raise careworn captives to trembling legs, weakened from their confinement. Taking the hand of one, she lifted him to his feet, but he could not stand. Legs buckling, Abby caught him.

"This one needs assistance walking, Noble. I'm going to help him out," Abby said.

"I'll help him," said a weak voice. Taking the man by the hand and wrapping his arm around his staggering cellmate, the two slowly made their way toward the soft blue light in the walkway.

"I have two that are barely conscience, Abby," Noble called. "We'll have to carry them out." Noble cradled a moaning frail elderly man in his arms and turned to exit the cell.

"Bring them into the walkway, Noble," Rue said. "I will leave sentries with them until help arrives. We can't carry them all.

Noble looked up to see two human like sword-wielding images positioned motionless on either side of Rue. Abby moved along beside of him carrying a young girl.

Staring at Rue, Noble asked, "Who is she, Abby? Is she a guardian?"

Abby smiled and replied, "Keep seeking, Noble."

The shadow walkers continued down the dark, winding corridor, opening cells. The deplorable living conditions caused many to be very sick, some even near death. Mortified, Rue placed sentries at nearly every cell.

The noise of the bars thudding to the ground stirred those who were able to stand. As faces pressed the cell bars, the soft glow of the Shadow illuminating the walkway met waving arms, cheers and praises.

"Stand back away from the bars," Noble ordered. "We'll have you out in just a second." With the thud of the bars, Abby shouted over the cheers, "Those of you that can walk help someone, if you can!"

Carrying a listless coughing child into the walkway, Noble asked Rue, "Do you think the prophet told us everything? We have opened a lot of cells and haven't found Abby's friend or my dad yet."

"I don't know. Try not to think about it, Noble. I know it's hard," Rue said compassionately. "Just keep opening cells. I pray that we find them soon.

"Shadow Walkers are coming!" echoed through the darkness, stirring hope from cell to cell. Lying flat on his back in the pitch-black darkness, Belor painfully rolled to his side and forced himself up to his hands and knees. Disoriented, he slowly crawled, feeling for bodies as he listened to the sounds that echoed in the darkness.

"Hey!" he said, shaking a shoulder he found in the darkness. "Did you hear that?"

"What," moaned a cellmate halfheartedly?

"Keller. Is that you? Listen," Belor said. A faint thud followed by voices cheering roused Keller to his feet.

"Help me to the bars," Belor said.

Feeling in the darkness, Belor found a helping hand. Racked with pain, he pulled himself up the man's arm. "The tormentors worked you over pretty good," Keller said.

"Yah," Belor affirmed in a tight voice. "Those little-round pry bars really hurt. My fallen brothers were really mad about something. And I think I know what it was."

Carefully, the cellmates made their way to the bars. Pressing their faces in the direction of the sounds, they could see a faint blue hue. Closing his eyes, Belor listened for the inner voice.

"It's Abby," Belor said. "She is near."

Hearing voices, Rue turned to see residence from the Northern safe house working their way down the corridor, attending the captives in the walkway.

"Help has arrived, shadow walkers," Rue announced as she continued to whisper.

Noble carried a motionless young woman into the walkway and laid her by a sentry. Hearing the good news that help had arrived met with mixed emotions.

"I don't think this one's going to make it, Rue. I can't feel a pulse."

"Rue! Noble! Abby! You did it!" came a familiar voice. Eben moved briskly down the corridor followed by more residence from the safe house.

"Eben!" Noble shouted. "This one's bad!"

Hurrying down the walkway, the young woman received quick attention and was transported to the surface. Pleasantries were put on hold as Abby laid another critical captive in the walkway.

"John, wake up!" Noble's father stirred at the sound of the young male voice. "Wake up!" Chela called, shaking him.

"Leave me alone. I hurt all over," John moaned.

"John. Come on," Chela said and continued shaking. "Help's on the way."

"You told me that already. Now tell me how many days ago it was you told me that, and I might believe you," John responded sarcastically.

"I already told you that I don't even know how long that I have been in here. You can't measure time in total darkness without a mechanical device. But, the tormentors' recent visit makes sense now. They never come down here except to bring in a prisoner or to feed us."

"I wish they would have skipped that visit. I feel like they broke every bone in my body."

"That's what I mean. They didn't bring in a prisoner or food. They came down here in a rage and nearly beat you to death. Rumor has it that they beat Belor too."

"Belor?"

"Yah. You know. Abby's friend. She's the shadow walker I told you about. And I just heard from the cell next to us that the shadow walkers are coming. Rescue's on the way!"

"Okay. Wake me up gently when they get here," he said, continuing the sarcasm. "And please don't shake me anymore."

"Belor!" Abby shouted.

"Stand back from the bars," Noble instructed. Abby was in the cell before the bars hit the walkway.

"Don't hug me, please," Belor said quickly.

"Oh!" Abby gasp. Belor looked horrible. Along with his clothes being shredded and charred, his face was red and swollen. Abby gently leaned her forehead against his and sobbed, "I'm so sorry, Belor. I'm so sorry."

"It's okay, Abby," Belor consoled. "It's okay. I'll heal. Get the rest of the captives out of here. Keller will help me to the surface."

Abby stepped aside wiping her eyes and watched them hobble across the bars. Turning away, she folded her arms and made a feeble attempt to compose herself. She felt an arm around her shoulder followed by a gentle squeeze.

"Come on," Noble said softly. He held her until she said, "Okay."

"John!" Chela shouted. "I see them. I see light. They're just around the corner!"

John raised his head and saw a faint blue light on the ceiling of the walkway through the bars. He forced his aching stiff bruised body off the ground. Steadying himself with one hand against the cell wall, and holding his ribs with the other, he shuffled stiff legged to the bars.

"I had given up hope, Chela," he said in a weepy voice.

"I know. When they first brought me down here, I soon gave up hope too. But then I realized that when you're in total darkness, hope's all you have."

John and Chela listened quietly to the shouting of the shadow walkers, the thud of the bars hitting the walkway, all mixed with the shouts and cheers of freed captives. As the blue light moved closer, the captives in the cell closest to the shadow walkers began to shout and waive their arms through the bars.

"John! I can't stand still. Freedom's so close, I can hardly stand it." Chela waived through the bars, shouted and cheered along with the other captives.

Finally, over the cheers and shouting, Chela heard a male voice shout, "I see empty cells! Where's my dad? Dad!" As the shadow illuminated the corridor ahead of the progressing shadow walkers, Chela saw empty cells across the walkway. He then saw a male figure carrying a sword and shield hurry past the corner to the center of the walkway and stop.

"Noble? Son?" John said in a surprised tone.

"Dad! Are you down there?" Chela heard the voice call loudly.

"That's your son?" Chela asked astonished.

"Noble! I'm here!" John screamed with every ounce of strength he had.

"Abby! Rue! He's here!" Chela heard Noble shout as he ran toward them. Light from the shadow entered the cell just before Noble arrived. John and Chela shielded their eyes momentarily. "Dad," Noble said with an excited tone of relief. He embraced the arm that reached through the bars toward him.

"Son!" was all that John could say, overwhelmed with emotion.

"Noble," Abby called.

Breaking the embrace, Noble looked toward the sound of Abby's voice, then back at his dad, and said, "Hang on, dad. We'll have you out in just a second." He rushed to the cell that he had past and assisted Rue and Abby. John and Chela then heard, "The gates of hell will not prevail!" the thud of bars, and the excited cheers of captives set free.

Noble buried his face in his father's chest and wept. The days of uncertainty concerning his father's plight ended with their embrace. John's towering frame leaned against the cell wall, his cheek resting on his son's head. In a place submerged in hopeless darkness, the soft light of the shadow revealed a man and son finding what they thought they had lost.

"I had given up, Noble," John sobbed. "I didn't think that I'd ever see you or your mother again."

"I would've never stop looking, dad," Noble said in a trembling voice. John kissed his son on the forehead as they continue their emotional reunion.

"Noble, we need to go," Abby said, as she stepped into the cell. "It's a long walk to the surface and John's in need medical attention."

"Dad, this is Abby. I wouldn't have found you without her help."

"Thank you, Abby."

"You're welcome, John," Abby said. "Come on. Give me your hand." Abby put John's left arm across her shoulder. John pushed away from the wall and Noble took the right side. "Your dad's a big man, Noble. I don't think that you're finished with my help yet."

John and the two shadow walkers slowly made their way up the winding corridor. Noble introduced his dad to Rue, who gave John a shock in her blue condition, and began to tell his story from the time he met Rue and discovered his clothes. When he finished, he asked his dad why he went into the woods and how he was captured.

"I saw the stream that ran across the farm and into the woods," John began. "And when I went to the vending area, I saw the path that led down the hill toward the stream and into the woods. I thought that there had to be a pond or lake down there somewhere for there to be such a well-worn path. So, I went down the path looking for a fishing hole. I noticed the wall, and was grabbed when I looked in the door. Once they had me inside, I was bound and gagged. I could hear you calling for me, but I could not answer. I was then taken straight to the dungeon."

"If you were grabbed and pulled inside," Noble asked, "how did your hat end up on the outside, in front of the door?"

"I don't know," John answered.

John, Abby, and Noble continued their climb to the surface with Rue leading the way, dismissing sentries as they passed, allowing darkness to return to now empty cells. When they finally surfaced, a large assembly was ready to celebrate.

MARION DAVID RUSSELL

CELEBRATION

CHAPTER 15

The celebration was not only for the shadow walkers, but also for the captives and the rebirth of the city as well. The people would be able to go back to their homes and businesses. The city could now go back on a schedule of town meetings, worship services, performing arts, etcetera, without constant fear of attack. However, there would be some that would prefer it to remain nasty, mean, and bitter—the sour grape crowd. But they no longer ruled the city.

The crowd cheered and shouted for the shadow walkers to stay and protect the city. "He will be back!" many shouted. Everyone agreed that Kuriopolis would try to take the city again. He only leaves for a little while. Rue calmed the crowd and began to speak.

"Until the city is on its feet, Abby has agreed to stay and aid in the ousting of the tormentors. She has nothing pressing on the outside and can stay as long as necessary.

"It would be my pleasure to fry a few more of the varmints," Abby shouted. The crowd cheered and the celebration continued. Noble and Abby exchanged goodbyes, and Rue walked with Noble and his father to the path at the edge of the city.

"Rue," John smiled, "thank you for helping Noble save my life." John looked over at Noble as he spoke. He could tell by the way his son was looking at Rue that he needed to give then some private time. He looked back at Rue and said, "I think I'm going to get a head start since I'm not moving too fast. Goodbye Rue."

Noble's eyes filled with moisture as he watched his father turn and start up the path. He was not looking forward to what was going to happen next. He turned to face Rue, knowing that this may be the last time he would look into those fiery eyes.

"It's time for your answers Noble," she smiled. "You asked me why I'd leave a safe house and help a total stranger. It's time you know.

Let me begin with the night we watched the tormentors from my window. I told you that night that some citizens very close to me were deceived by Kuriopolis and became tormentors. Those citizens were once guardians of the city, helpers of the people, just like I'm a guardian and helped you. They were once my friends, what you might call extended family in your world. Knowing that I'd have to help destroy them broke my heart.

But, that's not the only reason I helped you. You see, we aren't total strangers.

"When you entered the city, I had entered just before you. When I told you that I had been to the outside, my assignment was a young dreamer. I met you a long time ago, but you first met me at the safe house. I'm your guardian angel, just as Abby's friend is hers. My assignment has been, and will continue to be, to assist and watch over you.

Guardians assist those who put on the armor given to them by the Higher Powers. We help fight the powers of darkness that would destroy both our worlds if allowed. Just as I assisted you in fighting the darkness in this city that you could see, when you pass through the wall, I will assist you in fighting the powers of darkness you can't see.

"So, you're going with me?" Noble asked.

"Yes and no," she grinned.

"You never quit, do you? Isn't this how we started? What do you mean, yes and no?" he asked, trying not to be emotional.

"When you pass through the wall, you will get your answer," she smiled. "Now go help your dad."

He could not get a word past the lump in his throat. They embraced and he headed out the way he came in, searching. Would he ever see Rue again? Up the winding path he hurried to find his father. When they passed through the large wooden door, the answer came to him. "Yes."

Grandpa leaned closer to Tommy. "Have you ever been happy and sad at the same time? Have you ever had a friend that seemed closer than your own family? Then you know how Noble felt at that moment.

"Now, young man, its time to sleep."

Tommy slipped into his sleeping bag, but his eyes were wide open. "That was a great story, Grandpa!"

"Thank you, son. Maybe someday you will have an adventure as great as mine.

EPILOGE

CHAPTER 16

When I began this story, my target was youth. I hoped that they would enjoy, as I do, stretching the imagination. At times, I have found that humor, music, and even imagination have helped me remember the Scripture. Of course, we need to separate the truth from fiction when application to life begins.

However, when dealing with youth, there are at least two other groups that need to be addressed: parents and leaders. Sometimes these individuals are the same, but not always.

The responsibility of leaders, is to let their light shine in such a way that others will see their good works and want to do the same, which is to glorify God. (See Matthew 5:16.) If they see our good works that we give God the credit for and do the same, this glorifies God. Another responsibility, is to teach principles that lead to godliness. This means that they have to know these principles themselves. So leaders pass light in two ways: teaching and walking (or lifestyle). They cannot make others walk their walk, but must inspire others to walk Jesus' walk by spreading the word and living it. The word without the walk is knowledge. The word with the walk is wisdom. Jesus is referred to as the wisdom of God in the Old and New Covenants. He had the walk and the talk and is our example.

Much of what is said about a leader can be applied to a parent. In my attempt to raise three children, I spent most of my time putting out brush fires, if you catch my meaning. I spent way too much time trying to repair damage when I should have been doing preventative maintenance. If I teach principles that lead to godliness and live these principles in front of my disciples (or children), then when it comes time for them to make decisions, they will be equipped to make godly decisions. Thus said, we come to our last group: those being taught (disciples, youth, and children).

There comes a time when, like Noble's father, we hear our disciples calling but cannot answer. Even though we want to, we know from experience that they must walk on their own. There is no way around the school of hard knocks for disciples. If you avoid it, then you're not one of his. You will never be the extraordinary person that God wants you to be, that Jesus died so that you could be, if you enter by another gate.

Another point for the youth to remember is this: parents and leaders are not all-knowing and all-powerful like our Heavenly Father. But we are alike in one respect, or should be. God limits his powers when it comes to our free will, and leaders and/or parents should do the same for their disciples and children. God watches as we *all*, not just disciples and children, make world record blunders. (I wonder if there will be a movie house in heaven showing stupid Christian videos.) We cannot do for them or make them do what is necessary to avoid mistakes. All we can do is equip them so they can do, give them a chance to get their helmets knocked off a few times, and be there to pick up the helmets.

I'd like to say that our story has a "happily ever after ending". But, Noble would not get to see Rue again. What do you think his choice would be? You might miss adventures like this if you choose the easy road. And you might miss Jesus. You won't find Jesus on the easy road. So my advice to the Nobles will be brace yourself, and do not miss anything God has to offer you. Your walk has just begun. As you gain experience in your walk, you will be able to look back and see that God has worked things out for your good. (See Romans 8:28.) But until then, take it from someone who is on the top ten lists of blunderers: take heart. If I can make it, so can you. God forgave even me.

The Beginning

ABOUT THE AUTHOR

Marion David Russell, "Dave", was raised in Southern Ohio. Both, Dave and wife, Ellen, are graduates of Kentucky Christian College, now a University, in 1981.

Dave and Ellen have three grown children, seven grandchildren whom were the inspiration for the Shadow Walker story, along with five great grandchildren.

Dave and Ellen live in Medway, Ohio, where they minister at Medway Christian Church.

SHADOW WALKER *CORD OF THREE STRANDS: TRILOGY*
SHADOW WALKER 1 – THE BEGINNING
SHADOW WALKER 2 – NOBLE'S LEGACY
Part 1 & Part 2
SHADOW WALKER 3 – ADVERSARY
Part 1 & Part 2

MARION DAVID RUSSELL

Please visit my Amazon author page for a
listing of all my books

MARION DAVID RUSSELL

Made in the USA
Columbia, SC
22 March 2022